"AND THEY'RE OFF!"

They were bunched in two parts along the backstretch. Julie could see Beau astride Bonnie in the vivid blue and white Deepwater silks in the center of the first mass. Then some began to lag and some to surge forward; by the top of the stretch it was a four-horse battle. Bonnie had the inside, Canary Feathers to her right, then Lambie Pie coming on strong in the middle of the track and Trinket settling down to her customary late blaze of speed. At the three-sixteenth pole, Bonnie began to move ahead; approaching the sixteenth pole she had a half-length lead.

Then the jockey on Canary Feathers began to punish his horse severely. The big gray bolted nervously and banged into Bonnie, sending her against the rail. Bonnie bobbled twice, losing stride for an instant, but then dug in and went back to running her heart out. A great cry was swelling from the stands, for it was obvious something was wrong with the splendid bay filly . . .

SUNBONNET: FILLY OF THE YEAR

Other SIGNET Books You'll Enjoy

Sunbonnet: Filly of the Year

by

BARBARA VAN TUYL

A SIGNET BOOK

NEW AMERICAN LIBRARY

TIMES MIRROR

SIGNET, SIGNET CLASSICS, MENTOR, PLUME AND MERIDIAN BOOKS
are published by The New American Library, Inc.,
1301 Avenue of the Americas, New York, New York 10019

FIRST PRINTING, NOVEMBER, 1973

        5 6 7 8 9 10 11 12

PRINTED IN THE UNITED STATES OF AMERICA

*This book is for Bev and Cindy, who asked,
"What happened to Bonnie after that?"*

Prologue

The Daily Racing Form

Dateline: Wicklow Downs, New Jersey, September 8:

A field of nine three-year-old fillies, including the two undefeated stars of the Eastern turf, Deepwater Farm's Sunbonnet and Manfred Fiore's Canary Feathers, has been named for the seventeenth running of the Bridal Stakes to be run here on September 18.

The Bridal purse is now worth $100,000, plus the stallion services that are the singular specialty of this mile-long trial for the distaff side. Despite the presence of Mr. and Mrs. Karl Wills's California speedball, Dottie B, and Lloyd Grayson's hard-hitting, owner-trained Petal, this year's Bridal is shaping up to be a two-horse race between the hitherto unbeaten amazons, who have somehow managed to miss a prior confrontation.

The credentials of this impressive pair read like entries from the *Guinness Book of Records,* accounting for two new track records set and two world records equaled, and place both fillies so far in front of the competition for the Three-Year-Old Filly of the Year honors that it is practically no contest. Since the Bridal marks the last of the three-year-old filly races for the year, should either of these two emerge the victor, she would be assured of the three-year-old crown.

Sunbonnet, the big bay daughter of Bold Ruler out of the stakes-winning producer Starcrossed, runs in the blue-and-white colors of Rollin Tolkov's Deepwater Farm and is trained by Montgomery Everett. She approaches the Bridal with six stakes to her credit, including the Forget-Me-Not, the Meadowlark Oaks, the Florida Rose Blossom, and the Walnut Oaks, and total earnings in excess of $375,000. She has been training and running exceptionally well throughout the entire season, and has more than met every demand that has been made of her.

Manfred Fiore's game gray Canary Feathers, ably trained by Kyle Klepps, is not to be trifled with either. Bred in Florida by the late Winfield Riley, she is by the Phoenix out of the good mare All Smiles, and was sold to Mr. Fiore at private sale late in her two-year-old year. She too comes to the Bridal with six stakes wins, including the Illinois Oaks, the Golden Susie Stakes, the Geranium, and the Burgundy, with earnings of close to $300,000.

These two great fillies were scheduled to meet earlier in the year in the Florida Oaks, but an eye injury caused by a flying clod of dirt in the Burgundy sidelined Canary Feathers for more than three weeks, and for a time it was doubtful whether she would race again this year.

As usual, Sunbonnet will be piloted by young Beau Watkins, contract rider for Deepwater Farm. This promising rider has racked up some sixty wins for Deepwater in less than eight months against the very best reinsmen in the East. His horses seem unusually willing—even anxious—to run for him, and it is a well-known fact that Beau Watkins and any horse are a combination to be reckoned with.

Earl Mariner has the mount on Canary Feathers. This fiery-tempered veteran of the irons has ridden the gray in five of her six wins this year, missing only the Illinois Oaks (at which time he was sitting out a twelve-day suspension), and is guaranteed to give Sunbonnet the proverbial run for her money.

It is also worthy of note that both fillies have run a mile in times equaling the world's record, and in doing so set a new track record at their respective race courses.

The rest of the Bridal field is headed by the West Coast star Dottie B, and is rounded out by Petal, Miss Gold, Me Oh My, My Dear, Lambie Pie, and So Is Me, who might possibly be running in a race of their own.

Chapter I

The horse was perfect.

In the many months she had known the great filly, Julie Jefferson thought, she must have said those words to herself at least a thousand times. Yet the fact remained, its truth became plainer and more astonishing as time passed; this marvelous beast called Bonnie was perfect.

Not many eighteen-year-old girls own a perfect horse!

I may be a tiny bit prejudiced, she admitted silently, leaning on the rail and watching Beau walk the filly down the track toward her. But look at her—a solid dark rich bay without mark or flaw, the highlights of mahogany flashing in the gloss of her coat, the skin sliding and rippling over superb muscles all meant for high-speed running. The prettiest of toplines with a beautiful crest to her neck, in fact, good lines all over, from pricked ears to neat hooves stepping proudly along the dirt. Elegant legs that could stretch out into a tremendous stride almost as long as that of Man o' War. So spirited that she almost swaggered, thrusting out her big head eagerly as she saw Julie waiting. And in the soft brown eyes, a real and lively intelligence, much above the average, and what was more, a genuine love for the slim blond girl who had saved her life and cherished her for so long.

She was one of the best and most successful racing thoroughbreds alive, too, but that meant less to Julie than her personality. She was Julie's friend first, and Julie's racehorse after that.

Beau drew her up beside the rail. "Mr. Monty says he'll be with you in a minute, and then he wants our princess here to work a flat mile." Beau caressed the arching neck. "Since the Bridal's only nine days from now, he says I better ride her from now on," he said a little anxiously, for he knew that Julie liked to be included in the filly's training schedule.

"Sure, he's right," said Julie. Monty Everett, her lifelong

friend and now her boss, was the trainer for Deepwater
Farm, and he was always right unless Julie considered that
he was totally wrong; in this case, he was right. Beau Watkins would be Bonnie's jockey for the seventh time when the
Bridal Stakes was run, and even though the big filly loved
Beau second-best in all the world, it was for the best that
she grew used to having him, and him only, on her back.
Julie stifled a sigh. Even these days of glorious sunshine were
a little gloomy if she couldn't sit on her courageous, wonderful, pampered horse.

"You'll be back in the saddle in no time," said Beau, his
dark face illuminated by a grin.

"What'd I say? I don't mind, honest!"

"Your face dropped a yard and a half."

"Oh. Sorry, Beau," said Julie.

"Don't I know how you feel about Sunbonnet? Shoo," said
Beau, sounding for the moment just like his father, who was
the head groom back home at St. Clair Farm and had taught
Julie how to ride. "Your job now is to think good thoughts!"

"Gee, I know that, Beau. I'm not disappointed in the
least," said Julie, and produced a mock sniffle of woe. "She's
looking great, isn't she?"

"And feelin' better than that. She tells me she's gonna take
the Bridal by four lengths."

"You always say that," Julie told him, laughing.

"No, *she* does. And Sunbonnet's never wrong."

Julie held out a single blue gumdrop on her palm. Bonnie
smelled it and then inhaled it, her favorite treat. "I suppose
it's all right for me to feed her now and then," Julie said.

A strong hand came down on her shoulder. "What's this,
Jefferson, giving candy to the livestock? Don't you know it
rots the teeth right out of their gums? Maybe you have a bet
on Canary Feathers?"

She whirled around and said, "You scared me, you oaf!" to
Monty Everett, who was tall and broad and lean and very
good-looking, and four whole years older than she was. "As if
I'd bet on the opposition, even if it was . . . was Gray Maj-
esty himself! Canary Feathers hasn't got a chance against
Bonnie."

"She's a very game big mare, Julie, and she's won as many
races this year as Bonnie has." Monty was automatically cautious when speaking to Julie about her beloved horse, and
curbed his natural optimism. It was a habit from their early

days on the track, when it had seemed that every time they turned around they were faced with a new danger to Bonnie, and sometimes to Julie herself. "Don't get your hopes up."

"I will too get my hopes up. There isn't a horse alive who's going to beat Bonnie, till she takes the Triple Crown and retires undefeated."

" 'Sides which, she told me she was taking the Bridal in a walk," added Beau.

"You always act," said Julie to the young trainer, "as though I'd shatter into little jigsaw pieces if Bonnie lost a race. It's about time you realized that I'm grown up."

"Yes, yes, child," said Monty indulgently, patting her bright long hair. Only the slightest blush on his tanned cheekbones gave away the fact that he agreed with her. "Beau, let's see you work that mile now."

He used the word "work" as it is always used in training: to denote something other than simple exercise, the daily morning "gallops." When the horse is asked to *do* something, it is called a work.

As he watched Bonnie turn and jog back along the track, he took his stopwatch out and held it in his right hand. "I'm sorry," he said aloud.

"For what?" Julie, staring at her horse, was a trifle startled at his words.

"For treating you as though you were still back in Ohio playing with dolls. I don't really think of you that way."

"I know, but you do worry about me being hurt, and it's silly. I can handle disappointment, Monty. I know she's going to lose a race someday, truly I do. I may even cry when she does. But I won't have a nervous breakdown over it. Let me have my fun."

"I don't mean to be a killjoy."

"Then stop trying to be my father. Dad never treats me that way, and never did even when I was five. And I'm not five now."

"I know." He cleared his throat. "I'll try to do better."

"Think of me as your assistant trainer, for heaven's sake. Not as a fragile, high-strung girl."

"Yes, ma'am," said Monty humbly.

"I'm a darn good assistant trainer, too," said Julie.

"I tell you that about once a week," he protested.

"Okay, then try to act accordingly. An assistant trainer is

tough. An assistant trainer faces failure with a firm jaw, un-flinching in the face of blighted hope and disasters."

"Right. Would it help you forgive me if I gave you a raise?"

"Maybe."

"You have it."

"You're kidding!" she blurted out, amazed.

"No, Mr. T told me on the phone just now. Seems every-body at Deepwater has been telling him how great you are with the horses, and somebody blabbed about how you sat up three nights running with Curious Cottabus till he was over the flu. So he wants you to have a fifteen-percent raise. I told him that I was a pretty worthy specimen too, but he said I wasn't nearly as pretty as you, and—"

"He didn't!"

"Well, no. I got a raise too."

"Mr. T is super," said Julie fervently.

Beau was galloping his charge easily down the track to-ward them, standing tall in his irons, ticking off the poles as he passed them, and reporting on their progress to his friend Bonnie.

"Well, partner, it's a mile for us today. One flat mile. Child's play for you, but it's boss's orders. There's the quar-ter pole, the green-and-white peppermint. As if you didn't know!" said Beau, chuckling to her. "Sneakin' up on the lemon one now . . . three-sixteenths *it* is. Come on, girl friend, he'll have the watch on us wire to wire, so we better get ourselves together and be runnin' when we get there. Red-and-white eighth pole comin' up."

As they galloped past the candy-cane pole marking an eighth of a mile from the finish line, Beau simply gathered his reins from the long easy hold with which he had been galloping and proceeded to fold himself neatly into the tra-ditional "monkey-on-a-stick" position. Less than a sixteenth of a mile before the wire, he held her to the pace just long enough to look to his right beyond the outside rail and make sure that Monty and Julie were watching. He took his right hand from the rein, threw a momentary mock salute in the general direction of the trainer and the owner of this wonder horse, and then buried his face in her wind-whipped mane.

"Okay, Bonnet, it's on you now! We'll break their watch this morning for sure."

Bonnie answered this vote of confidence with an overall

burst of power that lengthened her already tremendous stride, and settled down to the serious business of running. The poles flashed by her in a blur of candy colors, and she reached for more and more ground with every stride.

"Hey, there, girl friend," Beau whispered into her mane, knowing that she couldn't hear him now but believing with all his heart that she knew he was communicating with her, "steady there, not too outrageous fast! We're only working out here today. You go too fast, you're gonna scare all those others off; then you'll have nobody to run with, and where will we be?"

They rounded the turn at the top of the stretch and virtually flew past the remaining poles. In the flawless rhythm of a superlative athlete, Bonnie sped under the finish wire, and Beau stood up in his irons and let the bay filly pull herself up as she pleased, easing her toward the outside rail.

"Nice move, Bonnie," he congratulated her with multiple pats and her special top-of-her-head scratch. "Your mama and your pal ought to be standing there this minute with canary feathers all over their faces." He burst out laughing at his own joke.

Monty clicked his watch and simply stared at it.

"Well? Well? Well?" said Julie, breathless with the happiness that came to her from watching her horse really eat up the track.

"Not bad," said Monty casually. "Made that move in thirty-seven, and I saw Beau take hold and steady her coming up the backside."

In the technical jargon of the racetrack, ".37" meant that Bonnie had run the mile in one minute and thirty-seven seconds. As Monty would also have said "She did it in thirty-seven" if Bonnie had gone three-eighths of a mile in that many seconds, the figure might seem confusing to an outsider; but anyone who had been working for a year at tracks all over the country, as Julie had, would know instantly what time was meant, judging by the distance covered. The fastest animal alive, the cheetah, can hurtle himself over the earth at fifty miles an hour for a brief while; but neither cheetah nor horse could do a mile in thirty-seven seconds. However, this shorthand way of speaking is often baffling to newcomers.

"She's training well, isn't she?" Julie asked him now. "Better than last time, even."

"I have high hopes for her," said Monty.

"Well, thanks for admitting it," said the girl tartly.

"I just gave you a raise and an apology," said Monty. "What do you want, a banana split on the top?"

Luckily Beau rode up at that moment, sitting tall in the six-pound exercise saddle and smiling with joy. "She sure worked that one easy. Did it all on her own, too, 'thout me giving her as much as an urgent word."

"Bless her little heart," said Julie, allowing the big soft lips to sweep up half a dozen gumdrops from her hand. "She knows there's a big stakes coming up and she's bound to win it."

"Right," said Monty, with some difficulty. He was really trying. Julie gave him a grin.

They walked back to the shed row, where Julie deftly removed the saddle from her filly and replaced the bridle with a blue nylon halter. Snapping a lead shank to one of the halter rings, she tossed the other end to Beau. "Hang onto her for me, will you? She's really not going to go anywhere by herself, but try to tell *him* that." The "him" was accompanied by a nod in the general direction of Montgomery Everett, trainer—as opposed, that is, to Montgomery Everett, lifelong pal.

Beau laughed. There was just no percentage in trying to convince Julie that "him" was undoubtedly right in insisting that someone be attached to the Deepwater star at all times. Perhaps she wasn't going to wander off from Julie, but the racetrack simply isn't the place to turn loose a $400,000 horse, even if it did belong to Julie Jefferson heart and soul.

Julie tossed a blue-and-white cooler over Beau's arm and began washing her beloved filly. Beau produced a couple of carrots from absolutely nowhere and started their morning game of take-the-carrot-out-of-my-pocket. Monty walked over and took the shank and cooler from Beau.

"Bandicoot will go once around today, and if you can find some company, try to gallop head and head. I think we'll breeze tomorrow if the weather holds, and I want her sharp, looking for a challenge."

The dainty chestnut filly Bandicoot appeared at the end of the shed, and her groom tossed Beau lightly onto her back.

"Right on, boss. Over and out," said Beau. "Come on, Cootie, it's you and me." He walked the filly away toward the track, engrossed in a one-sided conversation with another of his four-legged friends.

"Beau gets along with anything he rides, doesn't he?" Julie remarked to no one in particular; then an impatient nudge from Bonnie caused her to add hurriedly, "But of course you're number one!"

The initial washing completed, Julie reached for the aluminum scraper and quickly squeezed the excess water from the rich, mahogany coat. Then once over lightly with a wrung-out sponge, "To erase the scraper marks and catch any drips," she informed the filly. She covered her then with the cooler.

"I'll walk her for you, Miss Jefferson," said a straight-faced Monty, and turned toward the shed with Bonnie in tow.

"No chance, Mr. Everett!" And she grabbed the shank from his hand. "*You* have a filly on the track, and eight more to send out before we're finished—and besides, she'd much rather walk with me." Monty relinquished the shank with a sigh of resignation to stifle his inner laughter. No doubt about it, you could not tease Julie about that one bay face.

Julie stopped by a pail hung on the wall. "Hey, Smitty, is this Bonnie's water or Fancy's?"

"Bonnie's." The shout came from inside one of the stalls. Then Smitty leaned out over the webbing of the temporary home of Curious Cottabus. "Mickey's done with Fancy, I think. Anyhow, she's watered off, and I already hung a fresh pail in her stall. Mickey's prob'ly outside washing her feet now."

Julie walked on down the shed, leading her dream horse. As she passed in front of the blue-and-white webbings that marked the stalls of the various Deepwater horses, she could not help thinking that they were among the finest thoroughbreds that she—or anyone else, for that matter—had ever seen; and how lucky she was to have the opportunity to work with them.

At the far end of the shed, which housed some fifty stalls, she stopped to say hello to Duckfoot Wilson, the cheerful groom who all but ran the horses himself for his frequently absent trainer-boss, Douglas Cross. "How's everything today, Duckfoot?" she asked. "Did your brown colt get over his cold yet? How did Shadow Box run yesterday? I haven't seen the paper yet—did your big horse get in today?"

"Whew! That's a powerful lot of questions first thing in the morning, Miss Julie, but I'll try and tell you what you're askin'. First off, everything's okay down this end o' the shed this A.M., and the brown colt went to the track. We'll see how he comes back, and if he ain't coughing, we'll go right on with him. Shadow Box got beat a whisker's worth yesterday, but he'll be right out front next time outta the gate. And as for the big horse, scratch time isn't till 8:30, and we were on the eligible list, so I won't know till then." He reached out and patted Bonnie's neck. "And how's this young lady today? Skeets said he saw her working out here a while back and she had wings on her feet 'stead of shoes!"

Julie smiled at her filly. "She did work well, Duckie; she worked the mile in thirty-seven and wouldn't blow out a match when she pulled up. Monty says he's so pleased with her that she'll walk the next two days instead of going to the track, and then we'll gallop her an easy mile on Sunday. That'll leave just five more days to the Bridal. And I hope that *I* can stand the suspense."

She walked on around the shed, exchanging greetings with the grooms, hot-walkers, exercise boys, owners, and trainers who were found daily under the shed; and as always, she was elated that to a man they inquired about her filly.

When Bonnie would no longer stop at her pail for a drink, Julie took one last turn around the shed and then returned the filly to her stall to groom her. Currycomb for loosening dirt and scratching the itchy places. Stiff brush to lift that dirt. Soft brush to polish. Rub rag over the top, pick out her feet and apply hoof dressing, brush out her shining mane and tail.

"Toilette completed, m'lady," she said to the filly. "Now I have to look after a few of the others, before I lose my raise, and my job with it. I'll be back later, and maybe you'd care for a bite of grass then?" She slipped the halter off the magnificent head. "You know, you're just about the prettiest horse that ever peeped through a bridle!" With this last note of praise, Julie hurried out of the stall and ran smack into Monty, who staggered back and asked, "Is it a bird? A plane? A charging rhinoceros? Nope, it's Julie Jefferson in a hurry as usual!"

Monday morning came at the usual time, and it never ceased to amaze Monty that Julie could bounce out of bed at 4:30 and begin where she had left off the previous day. A brief stop at the track kitchen for coffee and a doughnut, a walk to the vending machine for Bonnie's daily box of gumdrops (Monty gave silent thanks that the chocolates always outsold the gumdrops, for he was far from sure that he could cope with Julie's dismay if she ever found a Sold Out sign in the gumdrop compartment at five in the morning), then up to the shed row, and the day began in earnest.

By the time Monty and Julie arrived, the shed was humming with activity. Sixteen horses had already been fed, their water buckets scrubbed and rinsed, stalls mucked out and banked, to be bedded with fresh straw after the morning exercise.

Beau greeted them in the tack room. "Mornin', Monty, Julie. How are you? Wondered if you want to change bits on Fancy today; she's been awfully fussy this week, no matter what I do with her."

"I know she has. Why don't we try the ring bit on her and see if it makes any difference?"

"Monty," Julie interrupted, "have you looked at her teeth recently? She has a rough set of caps in the back; maybe that's what's making her so irritable."

"No, I haven't. I'll catch Dr. McMahon this morning, and we'll have him check her. Scratch the ring today, Beau—in fact, we'll just let her walk until Doc gets here."

Julie went into Bonnie's stall and at once put her head out to ask, "Can we do Bonnie first today? She says she'd like to stretch her legs, and sees no reason to wait."

"Delighted to oblige her precious ladyship," said Monty, with what he believed to be a courtly bow. "Do ask her if two miles easy would suit her. If not, she'll have to do it anyhow, so try to make it sound appealing. Make her think it was her idea."

Julie dusted Bonnie off quickly, with a running monologue as she worked. "You know and I know that you don't care *how* far you go, and that smart guy out there is just being wise because he knows it too. . . . Quiet Morning is to go two miles today too, and I was going to do her, so how'd you like some company out there?" She leaned into the shed row and called, "Monty!" then jerked back, startled, as he appeared from the adjacent stall, practically nose-to-nose with her.

"Madame called?"

"Yes, and you can cut the hilarious comedy. Can I take Quiet Morning along with Bonnie and Beau?"

"Sounds good to me—for that matter, the pair of them can

go three miles tomorrow. Oh, and Julie . . . don't get hurt out there." He ducked barely in time to miss the rubber currycomb that sailed past his head.

As the girl and the jockey went out to the track, Monty sat down in the tack room to mark his work chart for the week. Provided there was no mishap, the various horses would work according to schedule; though he, like any horseman, realized that a misstep or a cough or even (he thought wryly) a hiccup could blow the best trainer's plans to smithereens. When he came to Sunbonnet he paused and chewed his pencil reflectively. Two miles today, three Tuesday, shorten to a mile and a half Wednesday. Thursday, a sharp three-quarters to be worked somewhere near 1.11, walk on Friday —and Saturday, he thought, would be D day.

"She's *right* now," he added half-aloud, "and it seems that she's getting *righter* with each trip to the track." He smiled at his jargon and made a mental note not to mention it to Julie. There was always the chance that the bay filly might get beat.

Monty did not even notice his own use of that particular piece of jargon; it is so universal at the track that everyone accepts it. In fact, if someone had said to him that Bonnie might be beaten, he would have had to think a second in order to understand what they meant. The phrase is "get beat," always and forever. And someday Bonnie was bound to get beat, but Monty could not envision the horse that would do it.

Unless it might be Canary Feathers. . . .

In several ways, thought Julie as they went to the track, this would be her great filly's most important race. Her mention of the Triple Crown had been simply an old stable joke between Julie and her Deepwater Farm "family," for only three-year-olds run in the Kentucky Derby, the Preakness, and the Belmont Stakes; and Bonnie, who would be four on the first of January, which is the official birthday of all thoroughbreds, had missed her chance at the celebrated Crown.

But the Bridal Stakes was terribly important too, if not quite in the Derby's majestic class. It was an invitational race —in order to run in it, a horse had to be asked by the track officials—open solely to three-year-old fillies. Only the best in the country were invited, nearly all of whom were in contention for Filly of the Year honors. It was quite an honor to be asked to participate in it, or, for that matter, in any invitational.

The most recent condition book published by the track, which gave the terms, entrance qualifications, and all other data concerning each race to be held during the present meeting, had told Julie that the purse was $100,000 guaranteed. This would be broken down to 60% for the winner, 22% for second, 12% for third, and 6% for fourth place.

"Sixty thousand dollars," said Julie to Beau and Bonnie. "That isn't a bad figure, is it, just for running a mile?" Then she shook her head and murmured "Man!" for she remembered the days, not so long past, when *six* dollars seemed a lot of money. These purses that Bonnie was winning were almost mythical to the girl. She had never really plunked herself down and taken the time to realize that they were real dollars, and that they were hers. Mr. T—Rollin Tolkov, Deepwater's owner—was handling her finances for her, and to Julie her raise of fifteen percent yesterday was much more real and believable than the $387,000 that Bonnie had won so far this year. And this was only September 13. The prize money was somewhere out there, important because it proved that her faith in her filly had been justified. The salary was here, though, and truly important, because it was evidence that Julie was working hard, learning well, and being conscientious.

There was another prize, however, beyond the rewards for win, place, and show, and this part had made her think hard and frequently. In addition to the vast amount of prize money, the first-place filly would win her owner's pick of a season to any one of three fine stallions; second place would take choice of the remaining two; while third place would be given the service of the stallion that was left. This added incentive was the reason for the name of the Bridal Stakes, which was also, Julie assumed, an atrocious pun on "bridle."

"If you win, dear," she said to Bonnie, "would you like to be a mother?"

Bonnie, who often appeared to sense when Julie wanted an answer, whickered softly.

"You'd make a really neat mama, that's for sure. And this would be a terrific chance, because Bothwell himself is one of the studs. Imagine a *free* Bothwell foal! But," she went on a little sadly, "we both know that I'd be out of my blue-eyed mind to breed you just yet, love. Don't we?"

Bonnie said nothing, looking wise. Beau did likewise.

"We do," said Julie. "You're running perfectly. Your wind is incredible, your stride's the best in racing, everything about you is in super shape. I haven't seen a sign of distress in you since you had colic that time when Stash trocarized you. And you *want* to race, doesn't she, Beau? I'm not sure that you'd be as happy as a mother as you are now. And I could ask you about that, but you wouldn't be able to tell me."

Bonnie threw up her head in the mettlesome, happy way that she had.

"So I have to decide for you, and I guess I decide No. Not yet. You'll run at least another season. If you win—sorry, *when* you win—we'll let one of Mr. T's mares have the service part of the purse. It says in the book that that's okay, provided the stud's owner passes on the substitution. And Bandicoot will retire in a few months, with a good record, and she'd probably do fine. So we'll say No thanks."

Beau looked at her. "Tune in tomorrow," he said, "same time, same track . . . let's get to work!"

The days alternately flew and dragged by, and before anyone was really ready, it was Thursday, and time for Bonnie's final work before the Bridal. All was going according to plan. Monty instructed Beau to back up the filly to the eighth pole and break off at the three-quarters, working six furlongs to the wire in the neighborhood of a minute eleven. The filly obliged by returning a brilliant 1.10⅘, after which she walked to the shed row, flanked by Monty and Julie. But as they were about to enter the shed, Monty saw the big gray filly, Canary Feathers, walking out of the receiving barn.

"You take care of Bonnie," he said hurriedly to the girl. "I'm going to have a peek at our competition." And patting his pocket to be certain that he had his watch, Monty set off at a run to the grandstand, to clock the impressive gray.

Canary Feathers had a powerful stride, not so long as Bonnie's, but formidable nevertheless. She worked five-eighths in fifty-nine (seconds, that is, although nobody at a track ever bothers to say so), and then continued, to gallop out a strong three-quarters of a mile in 1.13, giving every possible indication that she was ready to give the Deepwater entry a real fight.

Monty strolled thoughtfully to the barn, where Beau was cooling out the filly. He told young Watkins about the gray's performance. Beau whistled. "Two seconds more than Sunbonnet? That's close. That's about too close to be pleasing."

"Well, all we can do is wait for day after tomorrow," said Monty. "Bonnie's as prepared as she'll ever be."

Julie joined them, and while she grazed Bonnie before putting her back in her stall, Monty and Beau headed for the office of the racing secretary, where the post positions for the Bridal Stakes were to be drawn at 9:30. Entering the office, they were confronted by a small mob of newsmen. Somehow, thought Monty, four men trying to extract opinions from you always manage to look like a mob.

"Did you see Canary Feathers work out there?"

"Yes, I did," said Monty.

"What do you think of her?"

"That's a lot of horse," said Monty carefully.

"She did the three-quarter in the same time as your Sunbonnet."

"Very close," agreed Monty.

"Could you give us your estimate of what the results of the race will be?"

"Bonnie'll win it," said Beau inaudibly.

"Well," said Monty, pushing his fingers slowly through his hair and trying to be both honest and circumspect, "Sunbonnet is ready and Canary Feathers is ready. I think it's between them. . . ."

"You have a few other good fillies in the race, too," said a reporter.

"Yes, but look at the odds. Look at their records. Canary Feathers is obviously the horse to beat. Both of them like a fast track. If the weather holds, if it doesn't rain . . ."

"No rain predicted," put in another man.

"Good. Then it seems to me that the track will be lightning fast; so then it will depend on who gets the racing *luck*. Post position won't have much bearing on the race, since it's only a nine-horse field."

"Then you're saying that Feathers and Sunbonnet are about equal, and if your filly wins, it will be luck?"

"I'm not saying anything of the sort," said Monty. "I'm only saying that the two horses are good and that I think it will be a very close race."

"What about you, Watkins?" a newsman asked. "How's it look to you? You've ridden Sunbonnet in half a dozen races."

Beau said, "I'm glad Canary Feathers is gonna be out there. Otherwise we'd have a dull run, way out ahead of

everybody." He blinked hard. "Seven other good horses, sure.
But Sunbonnet is carryin' the same weight as Feathers, top
weight. That means the racin' secretary looked over all the
records of everybody and figured that these are the two best
fillies, which they are. I'm sorry if I sound cocky."

They all chuckled. "You sound like a man with confidence
in his mount," one said.

"That, I got." Beau nodded. "And you can say that in the
paper if you want to."

Then the assistant racing secretary began to draw the post
positions, announcing them as he did so. When it was over,
the two men from Deepwater Farm walked back to tell Julie
the news. "Sorry, Mr. Monty," said Beau. "Should have kept
my mouth shut in there."

Monty shook his head. "You were okay, Beau. Just imagine
if Julie'd been there. 'My Bonnie's the greatest horse in the
world!' And she'd have been baffled if I told her that was
laying it on a little thick."

"She *is* the greatest horse in the world," said Beau, very
loyal.

"Weelllll," said Monty, "one of the greatest, anyhow. But
so is Feathers." He thought. "Tomorrow Bonnie walks. She's
in fine shape. . . . Don't tell Julie, but I think she'll take the
Bridal."

"Why not tell Julie? Man, Monty, you keep treatin' her
with silk gloves, as if she's a yearling. You forget how she
faced up to a murderin' crook and took his gun away from
him when she had to save Bonnie? You forget how she
tamed that trainer that tried to steal her horse, or how she
held together like steel when Bonnie was dying from colic?"

"Right on," said Monty, ashamed. "I'll tell her, then."

The next day, the following chart appeared in the paper.

POST POSITION	HORSE	TRAINER	OWNER	JOCKEY	PROBABLE ODDS
1	Miss Gold	W. Nichols	Bellvue Stud	J. Simms	10-1
2	Canary Feathers	K. Klepps	M. Fiore	E. Mariner	8-5
3	Me Oh My	W. Kelley	S. Wilson	M. Greer	20-1
4	My Dear	Owner	L. Grayson	L. Hutto	4-1
5	So Is Me	S. Calvin	B. Appel	C. Trimble	25-1
6	Sunbonnet	M. Everett	Deepwater Farm	B. Watkins	6-5
7	Dottie B	L. Joshua	K. Wills	M. Steuwe	5-2
8	Petal	M. Whalley	Kaintuck Farm	H. Hayes	3-1
9	Lambie Pie	J. Cannon	T. Simpson	R. Molony	6-1

Chapter II

The morning of the Bridal Stakes dawned clear and warm, with clouds like tiny puffballs scattered across the calamine-blue sky. The smallest of breezes moved playfully along the turf, hardly ruffling its cropped blades. Monty looked from north to south, east to west, and decided that Bonnie could not have had a more suitable day for running.

He sent her to the track under Beau, to loosen up by jogging a half-mile and galloping a half. Shortly Beau reported back with the news that the filly was on her toes.

"Of course she is," said Julie, coming to cool out her horse. "She *knows* she's running today." And indeed she seemed to know, as she threw up her head skittishly and rolled her eyes at the girl.

When Bonnie was ready to be put (obviously against her own wishes) into her stall, Monty checked her over thoroughly and carefully. Standing up at last, he said, "She's in perfect shape. I think she's the soundest horse I've ever seen! I really believe she's going to win today." He eyed Julie. "Does that satisfy you?"

"You didn't mention her beautiful brown eyes," said Julie, and led her filly into the barn. Monty stood there with a you-can't-win expression until she reappeared, stood on tiptoe, kissed him on the cheek. "Thank you, dear Monty. That was very nice of you."

" 'S okay," Monty growled.

"Did it hurt much?" she asked, solicitous, and was turning to fly away from his outraged swat when Beau came around the corner with a fresh copy of *The Daily Racing Form.*

"Story in here," he said, "sort of hints that Sunbonnet might be the probable victor. Thought you'd like to see how they get it all together."

Julie and Monty put their heads together over the article. After a short history of the Bridal Stakes, a rundown of the entrants was presented, in the order of post position.

Miss Gold, a chestnut filly, with three wins to her credit this year for a total of $100,000. She will be carrying 112 pounds and is listed at 10–1 on the morning line.

Canary Feathers, gray filly, has won six stakes and $300,000 this year. She is weighted at 126 pounds and is 8–5 on the morning line.

Me Oh My, bay filly with a reputation for blinding early speed. The winner of seven races this year, but the Bridal is her first stakes attempt. Total earnings amount to $29,000, she will be carrying 108 pounds, and is 20–1 on the morning line.

My Dear, chestnut filly, winner of nine races (four of which were stakes) and $131,000. Weighted at 118, she is 4–1 on the morning line.

So Is Me, the outsider in the race. A roan filly, winner of six races and five times stakes placed, but never has been this distance before. She has earned $51,000 this year and is a longshot at 25–1 on the morning line despite her light impost of 107 pounds.

Sunbonnet, bay filly, winner of six stakes this year and $387,000. Shares top weight of 126 pounds with Canary Feathers and is the slight favorite on the morning line at 6–5.

Dottie B, a California horse shipped East just for this race. She is a bay filly, winner of eight races (four stakes) and $210,000. She is the West Coast "star" weighted at 120 and well thought of on the morning line at 5–2.

Petal, another hard-knocking filly, bay, winner of nine races (five stakes), but in lesser company. Unlike So Is Me, she has run this distance before; has earned $70,000, will carry 118, and is 3–1 on the morning line.

Lambie Pie, a brown filly, standing barely fifteen hands. The winner of ten races (three stakes) and $62,000. She will carry 116 pounds, and this is her first time in such company, but someone thinks well of her, since she is 6–1 on the morning line.

Julie said, "Six to five. They *do* think she's going to win."

"They have reason to," said Beau. "They have stopwatches and sense, just like us."

"Funny though, they didn't mention her beautiful brown

eyes," said Monty, and escaped with dignity as Julie was
looking for a stone to throw at him.

The hours before the Bridal Stakes were filled with the
usual hectic activity for Julie, and dragged just as slowly past
as such hours always did. Sometimes it seemed to her that the
more work there was to accomplish prior to a race, the more
time there was to fidget. "Makes no sense," she said to Bonnie, panting, "but there it is. Any other time I'd do this much,
it would be midnight by now." However, at long last the moment was there when Julie, on the lead pony, who was a
little black-pointed dun named Skittycat, conducted Bonnie
and Beau to the post.

The weather had remained flawless, the track was fast.
Bonnie herself was in marvelous spirits, keen and playful,
nudging Skittycat and trying her best to make him play with
her. "You be serious," Beau said to her. "You got a race to
take, gumdrop."

All nine fillies entered the gate in orderly fashion. It was
as well-behaved a lot of contenders as Julie had ever seen.
From the point of vantage she had chosen, sitting tall in
Skittycat's saddle, she saw the crowd surge closer to the rail,
watched the flag raised, and heard the boom of the announcer's call of the race.

"They're off! Going to the front is Me Oh My, showing
early speed, with My Dear and So Is Me ranging up on the
outside. Canary Feathers and Sunbonnet are in the second
flight, with Petal, Dottie B, and Lambie Pie in the third. A
gap of two lengths, and it's Miss Gold bringing up the rear.
Going into the clubhouse turn, the field remains as is.
Straightening out and moving up the backside, Canary Feathers makes a run on the outside. Sunbonnet is now making her
bid from the inside, with Me Oh My still maintaining a two-
length lead."

"Come on, Bonnie," Julie whispered into the great roar of
noise.

"Leaving the three-eighths pole, Canary Feathers moving
up on the outside, passing My Dear. Sunbonnet, moving on
the inside, is checked by a badly stopping So Is Me as they
leave the half-mile pole. Lambie Pie is starting her bid on the
outside; a gap of three lengths, and it's Petal and Dottie B,
with Miss Gold trailing."

"Come on, Bonnie!" shouted Julie, her hands entangled in
Skittycat's mane.

"Coming to the quarter pole, it's Canary Feathers head-and-head with Me Oh My. Sunbonnet, finding racing room along the rail, is making a belated run at the leaders. Moving to the head of the stretch, the field remains the same. Now coming to the eighth pole, Me Oh My is tiring. Sunbonnet, moving between Me Oh My and Canary Feathers, bumps Canary Feathers slightly, and Lambie Pie is moving fastest of all coming through the stretch. Leaving the sixteenth pole, it's Sunbonnet on the inside with Canary Feathers and Lambie Pie."

"Come on, Bonnie girl!" screeched Julie, standing up in her irons.

"Coming to the wire, it's Canary Feathers, Sunbonnet, and Lambie Pie beginning to hang. They cross the wire like that," finished the announcer. "The judges will examine a photograph before posting the order of finish."

"Oh, Bonnie," said Julie in mixed fear and hope, "if that twenty-five-to-one roan outsider hadn't got in your way, you'd have cinched it!" She cantered over to the unsaddling area to wait for Beau. The horses had pulled up and were heading there, where the jockeys would remove the saddles from all except the three possible winners. A sweat-soaked Beau on a wet-looking Bonnie found her and shook his head as she burst into questions.

"Too close to call," he said. "We were all right there. This is one time I can't say for sure that she took it."

Julie handed him her handkerchief to get the salt moisture out of his eyes. "You rode a terrific mile anyway, Beau. I wish Stash could have seen it."

He grinned. "Rather Dad saw me breezin' in ten lengths ahead of everybody."

"That'll be next time," said Julie.

Meanwhile, the judges were reviewing the photo, and now declared Bonnie the unofficial winner, with Canary Feathers second, Lambie Pie third, and Me Oh My fourth. Miss Gold had been fifth, My Dear sixth, Dottie B seventh, and Petal eighth; So Is Me had been eased, that is, allowed to coast in at her own choice of speed.

The first four numbers were posted. Beau, handing the soppy handkerchief to Julie, said lightly, "Well, see you in the winner's circle," and walked Bonnie off in that direction.

A valet took Skittycat from her so that she could follow her filly.

But the rider of Canary Feathers had a different notion. Earl Mariner was a veteran jockey, taller than most of his fellows but so thin that he looked as if he could fall through a flute without striking a note. He was made of rawhide and spring steel, and he had hands that could gentle a horse or haul it to a sitting position from a dead run. He also had one of the most fiery tempers in the business.

As soon as he had weighed out, he informed the clerk of scales that he wanted to call a foul against the unofficial winner, Sunbonnet, for interference leaving the eighth pole. "Inquiry" was at once posted on the tote board, and Beau, waiting atop Bonnie beside the winner's circle, was summoned to appear with Mariner before the stewards. Julie, dismayed but poker-faced, snapped a lead shank onto her filly's bit and talked soothingly to her as the vast crowd roared and chattered and buzzed with speculation.

"It's all right, Bonnie, you didn't do anything wrong. I know you're used to having your picture taken right away," said the girl, "and I can't *imagine* why they're waiting, but you just have to be patient. There's my good little girl."

Bonnie rested her chin on Julie's shoulder and sighed wetly.

The stewards of the track, together with both jockeys and both trainers, were watching the instant-rerun tape of the race. "See there?" demanded Earl Mariner, as Bonnie, moving up between Me Oh My and Canary Feathers, bumped the big gray slightly. "Don't tell me that wasn't deliberate!"

"Replay it," ordered a steward. It was shown again. The men looked at one another. "No," said the man who had spoken, "I see no foul there at all. You're wrong, Mariner."

Beau let out a long breath of relief.

Mariner glared at him. "Okay, Watkins. But the next time you and that bay thing get in my way, watch out." He stormed from the room.

Beau, on their way to the winner's circle, told Monty, who hadn't heard Mariner's remark, what had been said, "And he called our great filly a 'thing,'" repeated Beau indignantly, in Julie's hearing.

The girl flushed angrily. "Who did?"

"Oh, nobody much," said Beau. "Just Earl Mariner."

"Thing," said Julie. "Thing, indeed! Well, his opinion doesn't matter a great deal to me," she said icily, "but if I ever meet him, I'll . . . I'll *snub* him."

They heard the amplified voice of the announcer suddenly

boom out above them. "The results of the seventh race are now official." Beau whipped up into the saddle, and Julie led Bonnie the few yards that brought them into the magic circle; and for the eighth time in her brief career, Julie Jefferson's Sunbonnet was photographed as a winner.

Then they all packed up and headed back toward Deepwater Farm for a very well-earned rest.

Chapter **III**

Near the center of the Bluegrass region of Kentucky lay Rollin Tolkov's enormous Deepwater Farm, which Bonnie, as well as Julie and Beau and Monty, now knew as home.

Monty assigned Julie the joyous task of seeing to it that her filly had a good rest. Bonnie was to "freshen up" for a couple of weeks, and because her value was increasing with every race that she won, it seemed a good idea to the young trainer to give Julie to her full time. This would make the horse happy, and keep the faraway look out of the girl's eyes, which, try as she would, Julie could never help acquiring when she was not with her much-beloved Bonnie.

"But you'll need me to help with the Cottabus," she objected halfheartedly, "and Sugar Candy has a cold. . . ."

"And I have an assistant named Dan Gibson who's a pretty fair hand with horses too," Monty told her. "It's common sense, Julie. The most valuable filly on the place is Sunbonnet. Take her over. Play with her. Gallop her an easy mile a day. Turn her out in the paddock and lounge around with her. It'll ease her mind and let her really relax. We're taking her back to New Jersey in October, and she needs all the peace and tranquility she can absorb till then."

"You're right," said Julie, trying not to bubble with glee. Her lifelong obsession with horses had culminated in the ownership of the marvelous bay filly, and the trust and friendship that had grown up between them was a constant pleasure, the most intense she'd ever known.

"After all," said Monty, "you work for Mr. T, Julie, and he has a big stake in Bonnie's future. He'll be sharing half and half with you in her foals; every race she wins adds to her potential value as a brood mare. So I think it's right that for a while you spend—"

"All my time with her," said Julie. "Neato!"

"As you say," agreed Monty, "neato. So get to it."

About the third day of this idyllic time, Julie was walking

down a gently sloping field of clover, near the trout stream on the south border of the farm, when she saw a man coming toward her. "I believe that's Leon!" she told Bonnie. "I haven't seen him for months!"

Leon Pitt was the foreman of Fieldstone Farm, which Mr. T used as his breeding center. He was a large, solid black man of about sixty, who moved and spoke with quiet precision; he was as gentle a man as Julie knew, with an encyclopedic knowledge of horses and racing, and he had raised Bonnie from her birth to the time of the Fasig-Tipton auction, where she had brought the record yearling price. Leon and Julie both knew, without ever saying so, that they would if necessary die for each other, or for Bonnie.

"Well, now," he said, holding out both hands to Julie, "how are the two nicest girls in Kentucky?"

"We're *fine*," she exclaimed, catching his hands. "Oh, it's grand to see you again, Leon! How's Mary Anne?"

"She's good, she sent you a slab of her cornbread and her best wishes." Mary Anne was Leon's wife, who baked the most succulent cornbread in the world. "I had to bring over a couple of yearlings, and thought I might stay a few days. Get reacquainted with Bonnie, visit with you and Monty. Brought you a little somethin', too."

"Besides the cornbread?" Julie smiled. "You shouldn't have, but what?"

"Show you later. Here, big girl." He pulled some gumdrops from his pocket and fed them to Bonnie. "She's looking fine, 'specially fine, Julie. Hear she ran quite a race in the Bridal Stakes."

"And you just know she's going to do even better in the Storybook next month."

"Nice to see her playin' in the fields; a change of scene does all of us good, even horses," said Leon. He ran his hands down Bonnie's legs, looked up into her eyes. "Top notch," he murmured. " 'Member how you 'n' me sat talkin' about her down in Southern Pines when you'd bought her out of a river and . . ."

Reminiscences filled the long stroll back to the barn; they put Bonnie in her stall and went over west to the trainers' cottage, where they joined Monty and his assistant, Dan Gibson, for lunch, eaten in the big sunlit kitchen. When the last cornbread crumb had vanished, Leon said, "You want to meet somebody?"

"Why, sure, who?"

"Sit tight and wait." He disappeared outside. Julie stared at Monty, who grinned. She looked at Dan, who whistled and eyed the ceiling. Then Leon came in carrying a small, plump bundle of short-legged, big-eared, black-and-tan-and-white energy. "My Sally had pups," he began.

"A beagle!" Julie shouted. "Oh-isn't-it-adorable-what's-its-name-do-put-it-down-so-I-can-play-with-it-is-it-a-girl-beagle-or-a—"

"It's a little lady, and if you'd like to have it—"

"*Would* I!" A pause of wonder as the puppy, set on its legs, took a long look at her and then came at a wobbly gallop to meet her. "You dear little critter," said Julie, down on her knees and elbows. The remainder of her greeting was lost in mumbles and squeals.

"I'd say that was love at first wink," Leon told Monty and Dan. They watched the girl go down onto her abdomen and receive an enthusiastic face-washing.

"Would you believe that this tiny child, frolicking on the linoleum with that furry watermelon, owns a jockey's license in the state of Florida?" demanded Monty, half-joking, half in earnest. "Would you believe that she once outdistanced me in a black woodland and subdued the toughest crook in Kentucky before I could catch up? Can you credit the fact that this cooing, grimacing little girl has outtalked, outargued, and outsmarted some of the hardest-minded men in racing?"

"Sure," said Leon. "You should have seen *me* when the pups were bein' born. I was about three years old for better'n an hour."

"What's the matter, boss," asked Dan, going down on one knee to tousle the pup's floppy ears, "don't you like dogs?"

"Of course I like dogs. I'm just not sure I'd care to be tripping over one every time I walked in that door. Oh, well," he said, shrugging, "if you really want her . . ."

"What? Certainly I want her. You have no idea," said Julie from the floor, "how much I've missed having a dog around. Oh, *thank* you, Leon! I was brought up with dogs underfoot. It's always felt sort of vacant around here without one."

"There are eighteen dogs of various denominations running around our stables at this minute," said Monty.

"But not living in my room, sleeping on my bed, being friends with me and Bonnie," said the blond girl, getting up and embracing Leon Pitt. "You'll love Bonnie," she assured the puppy, who was looking up into her face and whining happily. "And she'll love you."

"I hope so. Bonnie isn't exactly crazy about Geronimo, Tonto, Blackjack, Captain, Patches . . ."

"She'll love this one," said Julie. "And I'm going to call her Nana, because she looks *so* responsible."

"That?" said Monty incredulously. "She looks like a live sausage."

"But a very responsible sausage," said Leon. "I'm glad you like her, Julie. I thought o' you when I first saw her get up and try to run. Spunky little cuss."

"I can't argue with that." Monty nodded. "They're a match, then. I now pronounce 'em girl and puppy."

"Come and meet Bonnie," said Julie, scooping up the blinking beagle. She ran out of the house.

Dan gave Monty a long sideways glance. "Boss," he said slowly, "it really isn't any of my business, but when are you going to tell Julie Jefferson that you're in love with her?"

Monty opened his mouth, but nothing came out that could be called words. Leon, smiling gently, added, "It's exceedingly plain to everyone that knows you, after all, except maybe to her."

"I never heard anything so ri-ridiculously ridiculous," said Monty.

"You're jealous of even a scrap of a dog who licks her nose," said Dan Gibson.

"Right," said Leon.

"No, no, no," said Monty, waving his hands. "I'm nothing of the type. I mean sort. No. Certainly not."

"Mary Anne was askin' me last night when you're gonna get married."

"Leon, she's a *child!*" said Monty shrilly.

"Yep, and Bonnie's a fuzzy foal, and I'm a college boy," said Leon Pitt. "That child's just about a woman, Monty, but you let her joyful ways fool you into believin' that she isn't. When you plan to open your eyes, and then your mouth, and ask her?"

Monty stalked to the door. He turned, hand on the latch, and looked at them both. "Maybe on her next birthday," he said in a miserable tone. "I don't know!"

"Well, if you don't, I will," said Dan. "She's the greatest

person I ever knew, and never mind if she does roll on floors with puppies."

"Right," said Leon.

"Oh, cool it, both of you," said Monty, and departed with as much dignity as he could muster. Leon and Dan grinned at each other, and sat down to another cup of coffee.

In the barn, Julie was holding Nana up so the beagle could touch noses with Bonnie. The great filly snuffed with suspicion. The pup whined. Then its tiny pink tongue came out and licked the enormous nose before it. Bonnie threw her head up and snorted. She glared at the fat little creature for a moment and then dropped her nose within licking distance again. She gave Julie a questioning whinny, which made Nana jerk with surprise, and Julie said, "This is our new friend Nana," and the dog kissed the horse one more time.

Bonnie put on an expression that may have meant "I'll put up with whatever-it-is if you say so."

Julie took the new pup outside to play. Somehow an hour slipped away, and she could never have told what in the world she had been doing all that time, but now the small beast was tired. "After all, you still are very young," said Julie, picking it up and walking home with it under her arm. "You'd better have a nap." She made a bed for it in the corner of her bedroom. Naturally, it ended up sleeping at the foot of Julie's own bed.

After turning Bonnie out in the paddock, Julie walked over to Mr. T's big house and in his four-room office in the west wing discovered one of his secretaries sorting the afternoon mail. "Small package for you, Julie, from Wicklow Downs."

"Oh, thanks. That'll be the condition book. I asked them to send me a copy as soon as it came out. Where's Mr. T?" She stuck the packet in her jeans.

"In France, buying something."

"A horse?"

"More likely a company."

"Talk about *busy!* I hope he can be back in time to see Bonnie win the Storybook." She sighed. "He loves her so, and he's had to miss her last three races."

"He says he won't miss the next one," the secretary told her, "no matter how busy he is."

"That's fine." She checked on Bonnie in the paddock, did a chore or two in the barn, cleaned her filly's tack, visited her puppy (who was still asleep, utterly worn out), took Bonnie in to the box stall and groomed her, talked to Leon learnedly about diet—Bonnie's, of course—and at last it was supper-time. The same quartet gathered in the cottage kitchen for this meal, and halfway through it, Julie remembered her package. She found it in her hip pocket, rather dented and crumpled, and opened it.

"What have you got there, Julie?" asked Monty.

"It's the new condition book, which might just include the Storybook data."

"Well?" said Monty, expectant.

"Well what?"

"What weight will she carry?"

She ran a finger down a page and did some rapid mental calculations. Her face told him. Then she said slowly, "A hundred and twenty-four. Good grief! That's as much as some of the older horses will carry, and it'll be top weight for sure."

"She carried two pounds more than that in the Bridal."

"Yes, but she's up against Trinket and Regula Goodun, and heaven knows who else, and they've been running *years* longer than she has. You know how close they came to win-ning the Walnut, and they gave her weight that time. Now she'll carry the same weight as they do. And if Canary Feath-ers and Lambie Pie start, they'll get in with a hundred and eighteen. It's not fair!"

"Let's see," said Leon quietly. She handed him the book. He flicked his eyes down the pages rapidly. "You're right, Julie. Here we are, Storybrook Stakes, a handicap for fillies and mares, three years old and up. The three-year-olds to carry one-eighteen; four and up, one-twenty-four."

"Yes, but—"

"*But*," Leon overrode her gently, "there's a penalty, three pounds extra for every race won since the first of September. So we take one-eighteen, the base weight for three-year-olds, and add three pounds for the Meadowlark Oaks on Septem-ber 2, and three for the Bridal on the eighteenth, and that's one-twenty-four."

"It isn't fair that she has to be loaded down with the same number of pounds as Regula Goodun!" Julie announced vehemently to the table at large.

"It is too, 'cause if they'd won since the date specified, they'd be carrying additional weight too. Of course, there'll be a couple of good horses scared away just knowing that

Bonnie will be in with *only* one-twenty-four, and they'll look and wait for a softer spot. You can too, but it's a shame not to let her run when she's in such fine shape."

"But Canary Feathers carrying only one-eighteen—"

"Is fair! Because she hasn't won a race since August."

"But—"

"But your old pal Leon no buts," he said, one finger aloft.

"I don't like it," said the girl decisively.

"I'm not wild about it myself," said Monty, "but it's the rules."

"The rules aren't *fair*."

"They are too," said Leon firmly. "They may cause a body some concern. They may make a young lady, who feels like she and her filly are one and the same person, kind of fretted and all red in the face. But they are fair."

"Am I red in the face?" Julie asked him, wide-eyed.

"Scarlet as a rooster's comb."

"My goodness," she said blankly, "I'll have to watch my moral indignation, won't I?" She breathed deeply and slowly until her face felt cooler. "Okay, then, she'll carry a hundred and twenty-four pounds."

"The stewards at Wicklow Downs will be overjoyed to hear it," said Monty.

"Don't you be sarcastic at my girl Julie," said Leon severely. But he grinned broadly. "Let's run this down now, see who we have to whip. There's Jennie J and Regula Goodun—they're impressive, all right, got great records, but both of 'em getting past the prime. Not far past, mind, but enough so I don't believe Bonnie needs to worry about them. Monty? Dan?"

"That's what I think," said Monty, and Dan nodded agreement.

"Trinket, now, she's a different story. She's a powerful late-runner, and only five. Healthy as a shoat, too, been runnin' all her life. Bonnie's gonna watch her close."

"But Bonnie can beat her."

"Yes. I do believe it. Then there's Canary Feathers, came in a mighty close second to Bonnie this week. She's a tough one."

"I hope Earl Mariner isn't going to ride her."

"Why, Julie?"

"Oh, he made a kind of threat to Beau after the race.

Called Bonnie a 'thing' and said she'd better not get in his way again."

"Earl is a hothead, like his daddy before him," said Leon. "That was just words. We can't wrap ourselves up in gloom and woe 'cause a man says words at us. Do that, nobody'd ever manage to be carefree in this world. Not in racing, anyway." He scanned the page in his hand. "Who else we have here? Lambie Pie. Well, there's another."

"We have to respect her, because she made a really dazzling move in the Bridal," said Monty.

"Right. That's three right there that you can't discount, Canary Feathers and Lambie Pie and Trinket. I think that's all the competition, though. Unless Bonnie gets badly boxed or something unlucky like that, I think she'll take it. The Storybook is the last big filly-and-mare race for the year, Monty; when are you plannin' to run her again?"

"Not till February. Or, there's the Bridal prize, though. Julie," he said, turning to her seriously. "Have you thought about that?"

"What, mating her? I'm not going to do it. Mr. T can have his pick of the studs."

"Probably for Bandicoot."

"That's what I thought."

"Kind of hard to pass up that rich prize," said Leon, "but I think you decided wisely. Bonnie has some important racing years to go, and I believe she's going to stack up a remarkable record. Remarkable!" said Leon proudly. "No other word for it, remarkable!"

"I love Leon," Julie said to Monty, "because he's always right!"

"Except when I'm wrong," said Leon. "Say do I hear a whine from your bedroom?"

"Oh, Nana!" Julie fled, to return in a moment with the pup frisking around her feet. "I thought she'd bark if she wanted me, but she talks so quietly that I didn't even hear her."

"Never heard that beagle bark yet. Maybe she only barks when she has something important to say, and nothing important has come up yet," said Leon, fondling the happy little beast. "Growin' like a bad weed, aren't you? Be a dog soon instead of a puppy."

"How does Bonnie take to her?" asked Monty.

"Bonnie adores her. But only I could tell it."

"In other words, the filly didn't break down her stall when you introduced them."

"You interpret me with cruel accuracy, Mr. Everett," said the girl loftily. "And Nana met Pushy and S'Mouse and Adorable and Foxy and Yiyon and even Corky"—these were all stable dogs except Corky, who was the stable goat—"and they all got along famously. Nana is going to fit in beautifully. Leon, how do you like Bonnie's chances to be Three-Year-Old Filly of the Year?"

"She just about has that wrapped up. And the Storybook will determine the Handicap Filly of the Year, so . . . well, maybe enough bragging is enough, hmm? But we'll see."

"We'll see a *lot* in that race," said Julie. "Now how about some lovely dog food?"

"I hope," said Monty, "that you're talking to the beagle."

Chapter IV

Three weeks before the Storybook Stakes, Bonnie was shipped to the track in New Jersey, Wicklow Downs, where she settled down to some serious training. The last three days at Deepwater, Julie had galloped her two and a half to three miles a day, and continued to work her at Wicklow Downs for another two weeks, when Beau Watkins took over.

"She's in the peak of condition, isn't she?" Beau demanded of Monty after the first working of the filly. "Razor sharp, and rarin' to go—have you ever seen her better?"

"Not ever. She's so good she almost scares me."

"Tell you the truth, Mr. Monty, I feel the same thing sometimes when I'm up on that saddle. It must have been something like that to ride Native Dancer or Big Red himself. Or Gray Majesty. As if a man wasn't riding flesh and blood, but . . . I don't know, maybe the wind. Or something like that. A *force*."

"A force of nature," Monty said slowly. "An intelligent whirlwind with a burnished coat. Yes. It is pretty uncanny sometimes."

"Then you feed her a gumdrop, and she's back to bein' a great horse again," said Beau, leading the filly away, "and you forget all that poetry stuff."

Monty chuckled, and went back to his work.

The days passed, and suddenly it was time for Bonnie's final "prep." Monty gave Beau his instructions in the rather gray dawnlight on the track.

"This is her last work, Beau. Let her go seven-eighths of a mile, and I want you to really let her move the last quarter." The Storybook was run at a mile and an eighth, and Monty was honing the big bay to razor sharpness at a distance just short of that.

Beau saluted and rode off, while Monty went up to the trainers' stand to join the clockers and watch her work. "Get the fractions for me, will you, Mike?" he said to a clocker.

It was one of those works during which Bonnie was inspired to see how fast she actually could go—when she combined her extraordinary stride and muscle power and her gallant heart with every bit of the art and science that she had been taught by a number of good men, and turned in a performance to make the boys on the backstretch babble for days. "What'd *you* get her in?" Monty turned toward Mike, still staring at his watch.

"Twenty-three and three, forty-eight and two, one-twenty-five and two; out in one-forty. And Monty," Mike added, "she's just working, not running."

"Thanks, Mike. For a minute I thought I'd broken my watch!" Later he told Beau, abandoning his usual caution, "She's ready to run the best race of her career." He even went so far as to repeat it to Julie at lunch.

When Mr. T himself turned up on the morning of the Storybook and asked how Bonnie would do, Monty restrained his assurance and said simply, "She has a very good shot in the race."

"She's spotting Canary Feathers and Lambie Pie six pounds each, I see."

"Yes, they're a lot of competition, and so is Trinket. But I have confidence in her."

"Good," said Mr. T, and shook hands warmly and went away to do some millionaire-style business on the phone before post time.

The sky was overcast, with a constant threat of rain, but none had fallen by post time, and Julie let out a relieved sigh. Her filly did not like mud, and fortunately had never had to race in it. After some minor trouble at the gate with Regula Goodun, who seemed to be jaded with her long years of bounding out of a steel box and pounding along a track with numerous other horses, the flag went up, the usual howl resounded, and the field broke cleanly and well and were off.

They were bunched in two parts all along the backstretch, and Julie could see Beau in the vivid blue-and-white Deepwater silks in the center of the first mass. Then some began to lag and some to surge forward, and by the top of the stretch it was a four-horse battle, with precisely those three horses that Leon Pitt had predicted would give Bonnie a race charging along beside her. Bonnie had the inside, Canary Feathers to her right, then Lambie Pie coming on strong in the middle of the track, and Trinket settling down to her customary late blaze of speed. They held this way to the three-sixteenth pole, where Bonnie began to move almost imperceptibly ahead, so that approaching the sixteenth pole, she was half a length in the lead. Lambie Pie was fading by now, and Trinket, on the outside, had passed her.

Then Earl Mariner raised his bat in his right hand and began to punish Canary Feathers severely. The big gray bolted nervously and veered left, tried to straighten, went off-course again, and banged into Bonnie, sending her against the rail.

Bonnie bobbled twice at the seventy-yard pole, losing stride for an instant, but then dug in and went back to running her heart out. A great cry was swelling from the stands, for it was obvious to the crowd that something was wrong with the splendid bay filly. Canary Feathers forged ahead, but Bonnie was right with her; at the finish line, the gray was in the lead by no more than a nose.

As Trinket and Lambie Pie came across behind them, and before Bonnie had come to a stop, Beau was out of the saddle.

Julie, from her point of vantage of Skittycat's back, urged the little dun gelding onto the track and galloped down toward the finish line, shaking with fear for Bonnie and anger at the sheer viciousness of the jockey Earl Mariner. She pulled up the startled pony, jumped to the ground, and dropped the reins over his head, leaving him ground-tied in the middle of the track.

Bonnie stood on three legs, holding her left forefoot off the ground, sweating heavily, the great veins in her neck swollen. Beau was soothing her with his hands and crying openly, the tears cutting down through the sheen of perspiration on his cheeks. "Oh, Julie," he said as the girl came to them, "she's game, just too game for her own good!"

"What's wrong?" Julie asked, distracted, wanting to touch the poor leg that Bonnie was favoring, knowing that she must not do it. "What's wrong with her?"

"I felt something happen to her when Feathers hit her. I don't know how bad. But she wouldn't quit! She was bound to win that race! She just would not quit!"

"Mariner did it. He was beating his horse so she'd bump Bonnie. He ought to be . . . Oh, something terrible ought to happen to him! Why don't they come and help her?"

"Track ambulance is comin' now," said Beau. "You mind

lending me your hanky?" She fumbled it out and handed it
to him. "Thanks, Julie. Now, don't you worry. She's . . ." He
could not go on. He was too full of dread for the great filly.

Monty was making his way to the clerk of scales to claim
a foul, his heart in his throat, while on the infield board the
"inquiry" sign was already flashing, the stewards having ordered it because the bumping had been so obvious. The order
of finish was posted too: Canary Feathers, Sunbonnet,
Trinket. The numbers of the first two horses were flashing.

Mr. T was sitting in his box behind the grandstand,
all but petrified with shock, wanting to go dashing down
onto the track, telling himself that he'd only be in the way.
Above the neat gray beard his lips moved in a silent prayer.
There was no selfish motive behind this—he was praying for
Julie's happiness, which would depend so much on what was
wrong with her Bonnie.

Manfred Fiore, the owner of Canary Feathers and the employer of Earl Mariner, was looking for the latter, in order
to tell him that he was fired.

And at home on Fieldstone Farm, Leon and Mary Anne
Pitt, who had been listening to the broadcast of the race,
stared at each other with apprehension and waited for the
news.

Julie stood numbly watching her filly as the track ambulance drew up. It was a large horse trailer, which sat very
close to the ground. The driver and a second man came
hurrying to Bonnie and began to lead her toward the gradu-
ated ramp. She looked at Julie and gave a muffled, demanding
whinny of fear. Julie sprang to her head and took her by the
bridle.

"Who are you, kid? What are you doing? This horse is
hurt."

"I'm her owner," said Julie. "I raised her . . . I mean, I
. . ."

"That's all right," said the driver. "You take her up, then."
Julie led Bonnie, hobbling on three legs, to the end of the
low ramp, and the filly hopped painfully onto it and, slowly,
into the trailer. With Julie on one side and the second man on
the other, Bonnie stood carefully balancing as the ambulance
eased off toward the shed row.

"The vet will be there when we get to her stall," the man
told her. "He's the best vet we ever had at the Downs; he'll
see to her good."

Julie looked at him over Bonnie's wet back. "Do you think her leg's broken? She finished the race, after all."

"No telling. Try not to worry."

"Yes," said Julie in a frozen, polite voice, looking at her horse.

The stewards were reviewing the tape of the race, and Beau came into the room just as the four leaders swept in two dimensions toward the three-sixteenth pole and the image of Bonnie began to draw ahead of Canary Feathers. He stood silently behind Monty's chair as the accident happened and the horses dived forward under the wire.

The stewards consulted quietly. Beau stared at Earl Mariner with no expression whatever.

"Canary Feathers was responsible," said a steward. "We agree on that. Her number will be taken down and placed second, for interference at the sixteenth pole. Sunbonnet is officially the winner."

"Look here!" said Mariner.

"You, Mr. Mariner," the steward went on coolly, "draw a twenty-day suspension for excessive punishment of your horse, causing her to bolt into Sunbonnet."

"That's great," said Mariner. "My boss just fired me."

Monty stood up. "If I could prove that you bumped her on purpose, I'd knock some of that temper out of you," he said quietly. Mariner glared at him; then, apparently realizing that Monty was twice as broad as he was, he scowled and left the room.

Beau and Monty walked outside. "Man like that," Beau said, "he doesn't need wallopin', he needs to be stuck in some kind of job where if he gets mad, there's nothing alive anywhere near him. Let him take out his tantrums on stone or paper or steel. Keep good horses and people away from him."

"So Fiore canned him. I guess that will make him think, if anything will. He's ridden for Fiore practically all his career."

"He's gonna have trouble riding for anyone else. He has a mean reputation. I s'pose," said Beau, trying hard to be generous, "that that's punishment enough for what he did to Bonnie."

"How did she seem to you, Beau?"

"Not good, Mr. Monty. Not good at all."

Sometime later, the Deepwater contingent, including Mr. T, was huddled around the Wicklow Downs veterinarian, who

held a fistful of X rays. Everyone there knew precisely how
fragile a thoroughbred is; everyone was trying not to antici-
pate disaster.

"She's shattered one of the sesamoid bones," said the doctor abruptly. "You all know what that means."

"What?" said Julie.

"No racing for a year. At least a year. Maybe no more at
all."

"Forever?"

"You can't predict these things, miss. Off the record, I'd
say in a year and a half, perhaps, if she's had really good
care, she may come back. That isn't a promise. It's an opti-
mistic guess. Nobody will know for at least a year."

"She's not in danger of . . . of dying?" whispered Julie.

"No, no, child, and I've given her shots that will sedate
her and take away the pain. Very shortly. When you get her
home—"

"Just a moment," said Mr. T. "I don't understand the
technical terminology. Do I apprehend that Sunbonnet's leg
is broken?"

"Well, not quite that. Unless you'd take it that a broken
nose equaled a fractured skull. See here," said the vet, choos-
ing an X ray, "this shows that she's shattered the left-upper
sesamoid. Above the pastern, and below the cannon, there
are four small bones called the sesamoids. Behind her ankle,
see?" he said, tapping with his finger. "It's unfortunate, it's a
pity that it happened, but it might have been much, much
worse. Believe me, I examined that filly from stem to stern,
and this is all that's wrong. Otherwise she'd never have finished the race."

"He don't know Bonnie," said Beau to Monty in a low
voice. "She'd have finished with all four coffins cracked."

"And with the best of nursing, she may be able to race in,
say, eighteen months?" said Mr. T to the vet.

" 'May' is the word. Not 'will' at this stage, but 'may' race
again." His professional coolness dropped for an instant. "I,
for one, devoutly hope so. This is a fantastic racehorse, sir."
He thought. "When she's mending, it would help a lot if she
could swim. Have you access to a horse swimming pool?"

"I'll build one," said Rollin Tolkov.

The other laughed. "Well, that's hardly necessary. There's
a new one at Shenandoah Downs that cost in the neighborhood of ninety-five thousand dollars."

"I'll build one," Mr. T repeated.

The veterinarian blinked. "Oh, I see. It's the newest thing in the treating of bad-legged horses, and it's superlative exercise for them; just one or two laps around a pool do wonders for the muscles. But for one horse . . . Do you own many others?"

"A few," said Mr. T. "Deepwater Farm is my place."

"Oh, my," said the doctor, "of course, you're Mr. Tolkov. I didn't remember that Sunbonnet's a Deepwater filly. Well, then, build your pool, by all means. You can recover the cost of it by renting it out to other owners, too—and that would be a boon to every small owner in central Kentucky. There's nothing like swimming to tone up bad underpinnings, without putting any weight to bear on them. I think your trainer here will be in charge of Sunbonnet till she's home? Then here's what I want you to do," he said, and began to instruct Monty in a recovery program, to be relayed to the Deepwater Farm vet.

Julie wandered into Bonnie's stall. She looked woefully at the great bay, who had stopped sweating by now and stood on three legs with a rather glazed look in her eye.

"You don't hurt, do you, baby?" Bonnie blinked listlessly. "You're going to be all right," Julie told her. "You'll have a long rest, and then . . . then you'll feel fine."

She went into the farthest corner of the box stall and faced the wall to hide her silent tears from the men outside.

"You will feel fine," she said, "you will! You're the best horse in the world, and this isn't going to stop you. That's a promise. If you can't be a racehorse, well . . . well, then, you'll be a mother, and I'm sure you'll like that just as much as r-racing."

From somewhere deep in her gallant heart, Bonnie found the energy and the courage to produce a very small whinny of love and gratitude.

Chapter V

"Julie," said Mr. T abruptly, as the baked Alaska was brought in and put on the table with a flourish, "have you given any thought to breeding Bonnie, taking advantage of the stud service she won in the Bridal Stakes?"

"Yes, I have, but I promised that prize to you," said Julie, "and you've already picked Bothwell for Bandicoot."

"Bonnie won it fair and square," he told her earnestly, "and I've decided she should be the one to be bred, if you haven't any objections. If you have, then let's hear 'em, because I'm going to argue you out of them."

She giggled. "That's a good way to start a discussion. I've already argued myself out of all the objections that I could think up. Mainly, taking time out for foals usually finishes the athletic endeavor." He nodded, and she went on. "But we don't know, and we won't know for over a year, whether Bonnie will ever be able to race again." After more than three weeks of living with that fact, Julie could now talk calmly about it, though now and then there were sad little pangs accompanying the words. "It's a foolish gamble to take, just to let her lie fallow—if that's the term I want?—not to let her be useful for what might have been her best year. So I think, when she's better, that we ought to take her to a fine stud farm."

"Monty?" said Mr. T, digging into his portion of the luscious dessert.

"Yes, I agree, but I thought we'd have to convince Julie."

"You don't credit me with any brains at all where Bonnie's concerned!"

"Yes, I do. But I was so torn between breeding her and waiting to see how she runs when she's better that I figured you'd be even more so."

"Maybe I was. But it's the only sensible decision." She turned to their employer. "I do think it's your right to send

49

Bandicoot to Bothwell, though. Otherwise, it's Indian-giving."

"That's one reason I asked you over here for dinner," said Mr. T, "the other being that I hadn't had a chance to sit down with you two for far too long. Why, you peel away thirty years for me, do you realize that? I feel young again, and walk with a spring in my step, and startle my associates by exclaiming 'Far out!' at the least provocation. I also want your opinion on a new Yo-Yo I just acquired."

"I'm a Frisbee man myself," said Monty.

"But about Bandicoot," said Julie, firm of jaw and ready to debate.

"She's an excellent mare, but her foals won't bring much more than a tenth of what Bonnie's will," said Mr. T. "And as half of Bonnie's production will be mine, it's only a matter of economics. And Bothwell stands at stud for such a high figure that I ordinarily wouldn't even consider sending Bandicoot to him."

"Is he so great? Bothwell?"

"Indeed he is. His stud fee is eighteen thousand dollars."

"Wow! That much?"

"And he's worth it. He has one of the best produce records in America. And he retired sound, with earnings in excess of nine hundred thousand dollars."

"His yearlings are nearly always the biggest and strongest at the August sales," Monty added.

"Bonnie should have a wonderful foal by him. All right," said Julie, spooning up the last puddle of ice cream, "we'll send her there when she's better. Your economics are sounder than mine, Mr. T."

"Which reminds me that you're becoming a rather wealthy girl," said their host. "Bonnie's winnings, gross, now add up to $493,000. After taxes and—"

"That's nice for Bonnie," said Julie. "It's *her* money, really."

Mr. T laughed. "Legally and practically, I'm afraid she can't spend a penny of it, even for gumdrops."

"Well, you can take the cost of the new swimming pool out of it. And Bonnie's vet bills."

"Her expenses, naturally; the pool, absolutely not. I'll get my investment out of that in no time. It'll be making money for Deepwater before you know it."

"Fine," said Julie. The whole matter of finances bored

her, though she tried to seem interested for Mr. T's sake. Once she had realized that she would always be able to provide for her horse and if necessary her father, she had lost all concern for the subject. What was important to her in life was friends and horses and dogs and other animals, in no particular order.

Monty was talking to the older man about Bonnie's treatment. "Five more weeks of standing in her stall, at least."

"Is the cast still on? Are you having any trouble with her growing restless?"

"Not yet; and yes, the cast's still on. If she does start acting up, and she's spirited enough to want to move around pretty soon, then I'll have to tranquilize her. I've cut down on her feed, of course. She seems in reasonably good spirits; both Julie and I think so."

"Good. When she's ready for exercise, the pool will be there waiting."

"You are *such* a good man," said Julie impulsively, "building a swimming pool for lame horses just because Bonnie's hurt!"

"Nonsense," said Mr. T, flushing at the compliment, "it's simply an excellent investment. Why don't you finish the baked Alaska?"

"I'll split it with you," said Julie. "There must be about a pint left, and that's too much for me."

"I'm on a diet," said Mr. T, "so give me a little less than half." He patted his bulging waistline. "How's that fat beagle of yours, speaking of diets?"

Nana was splendid. She was growing a little every week, and while having the run of Deepwater's five thousand acres, always managed to get back to Julie's room in time for supper and another night across the foot of the girl's bed. Her sole flaw was that in no way could she be persuaded to bark. "A beagle is born to bark," Julie told her frequently, but Nana only whined or gave a small yip for answer.

Rather to Julie's surprise, the pup and the great bay filly had become pals. Nana was frequently discovered asleep in Bonnie's straw, in danger of being accidentally stepped on and squashed; but the horse seemed to take care where she put her hooves when the dog was nearby.

Bonnie's eight weeks of complete inactivity were over on Christmas Day. That morning Monty decided that she could be hand-walked for the first time, and Julie led her with a shank, once around the big broad aisle that encircled the sixty stalls, quite slowly and cautiously, and then back into her tiny home to rest for another twenty-four hours. She favored her left foreleg, naturally—putting very little weight on it and hopping three-footed most of the way—and she was suspicious of the special shoe she'd been shod with, but when it was over, Bonnie seemed as relieved as Julie was to discover that she could still get herself from place to place.

There was a grand Christmas dinner in the dining room of Tolkov's enormous house. There for the day were Julie's father, Rand Jefferson, and Monty's, Will Everett. There were Beau and his dad, Stash. There were Leon and Mary Anne Pitt, and Dan Gibson and his uncle, the ex-trainer Rodinbaugh, who had once ("back in his misguided days," as Julie put it) tried to buy Bonnie illegally, and who now worked for Jonas Black. There was Irv Blaise, Deepwater's top jockey, and several other jockeys, and the resident vet, and Mr. T's two secretaries, and ten or twelve other people to add to the jolly din. And there were more turkeys than anyone bothered to count; and as for the mashed potatoes, they would almost have filled the new swimming pool.

The aforesaid jolly din was, of course, almost all talk about horses, for everyone there except Julie's father had been intimately connected with racing for most of his or her life. Much of the talk, too, was about Bonnie, and so many questions were asked in that quarter that finally Mr. T insisted on Monty's standing up and making a speech, sprinkled with technicalities about icing of legs and multiple X rays and diets, that outlined everything that had been done for the filly and projected everything that would be done.

After dinner Mr. T wisely allowed everyone to roam around his two living rooms, splitting into family groups, mixing with old friends, catching up on family news and chattering incessantly. Rand and Julie slipped away after a while and went out to feed Bonnie a huge Christmas carrot. Nana emerged sleepily from the straw beside Bonnie's hoof and was introduced to Rand Jefferson, with whom she struck up an immediate friendship.

And too soon it was over and everyone was scattering to their own homes, and Julie fell onto her bed and held Nana aloft and said happily, "Bonnie *walked* today!" and then they both fell asleep.

It was not until the following day that she discovered via

The Daily Racing Form that Sunbonnet had been named not only Three-Year-Old Filly of the Year but also Handicap Filly of the Year. It would have made, she thought a bit sadly, a wonderful announcement to make to the assembled throng on Christmas. They were both really meaningful honors, and would boost Bonnie's reputation as well as the price of her foals.

But ultimately they only reminded her that Bonnie would not be racing for a long time, perhaps forever; and she went to her room and cried briefly into Nana's warm, round little side.

Then she dried her eyes and went out to walk Bonnie again.

By New Year's Day, the filly's official fourth birthday, she was venturing outside for a few minutes. In the following weeks she alternated between swimming around the gigantic special pool, which she appeared to enjoy, and soaking up the cool Kentucky sunlight in a small round "sun paddock" that allowed her no room to break into an impulsive run.

Slowly, ever so slowly, Bonnie began to trust more weight on her left fore. And the X rays showed a gradual knitting that was most encouraging. But no one could say anything definite one way or the other about her future running ability.

Then it was February, and time for her to be put in a van and taken gently and carefully over to Greyhill Stud, where the mighty Bothwell lived.

It was only two hours from Deepwater Farm, even at the cautious pace of Tolkov's best driver. Julie rode in back with her filly, at Monty's suggestion; as did Nana, definitely not at Monty's suggestion. "We'll both keep an eye on you, dear," Julie said to the horse as they got under way, "and you must try to balance very cleverly, and not shift around." But Bonnie had been tranquilized, and rode out the journey staring into space and batting her eyelids drowsily.

The van stopped at the office of the Greyhill Stud Farm and Julie went in to sign papers and show her credentials and, in short, prove who she was and how she happened to be bringing in a filly, after which the man on duty gruffly directed her driver how to reach the barren-mare barns, where Bonnie would be housed. Julie got back in with her beasts, and they trundled up and down the road till they came to the filly's temporary home.

The barns were large and as cleanly kept as Deepwater's

own, and the setting was beautiful: broad fields dedicated to the basic ingredients of hay, uncountable paddocks protected by white board fences, and here and there a grazing or sunning horse. So far, so good, thought Julie, glancing up as a pheasant went noisily by. She picked Nana off the ground and popped her back into the van, led Bonnie tenderly down the ramp, picked up Nana and put her back inside, said hello to a tall man with a heavy moustache who had just come out of the nearest barn, snatched up Nana and inserted her in the van, put up the ramp and closed the door firmly on a whimpering beagle.

"This is Sunbonnet," said the tall man, not as a question, but as though he were informing Julie of something she didn't know. "How's her leg?"

"Coming along nicely, but she—"

"Did Everett send the vet's instructions?"

"Yes. Here," said Julie, fishing them out of her jacket and handing them over. "Her exercise is—"

"Don't worry, we know how to take care of cripples," said the man, stuffing the paper into his jeans. "Bring her in." He turned his back and walked into the barn.

"I'm Julie Jefferson," said the girl, following with Bonnie. "Sunbonnet's owner."

"I know." Then, as if reluctant to divulge his own identity, he added, "Robert Lenkes. I'm manager of Greyhill."

He led her to a stall that was so fresh and clean that it almost sparkled. Bonnie went in obediently. It struck Julie that she would not be seeing the filly for a while, and a terrible sense of loss swept her. "When will you breed her?"

"Hard to say, Miss Jefferson. Not before March."

"That long?"

Lenkes heaved an audible sigh. "Normal breeding season is March to first of July. You ought to know that."

"Yes, I—"

"A maiden mare is always brought in early, to settle down and become acclimated." He sounded like a man reading from a primer that bored him. "She'll be well taken care of, and her own veterinarian's instructions followed to the letter." He looked at Bonnie for a moment. "She's a fine horse. Impressive record. It was a dirty break she got at Wicklow Downs. I'd sure never let Earl Mariner sit on one of *my* bangtails," he said, sounding more human.

He's not nasty, he's only gruff, Julie told herself. "Can I see Bothwell before I leave?" she asked.

"He's in his paddock. I'll show you." Lenkes moved off briskly, so that Julie had only a few seconds in which to tell Bonnie good-bye. Outside, he pointed to a large fenced enclosure. "I'll ask you to leave after you've looked him over, Miss Jefferson. This is a busy place, and we don't have time to shepherd strangers around." He glanced down at her; his eyes were cool but not unpleasant. "You understand?"

"Oh, sure, I work for Deepwater Farm, after all."

"Then you know you shouldn't try to get too friendly with a stallion," he said, and walked off.

Julie, after telling her driver that she'd be right back, ran over to the exercise paddock. She stood on the lowest board of the fence, and Bothwell took her breath away.

He was huge for a thoroughbred, at least seventeen hands high, a dark brown horse of regal bearing and magnificently proportioned despite his impressive size. His muscles bulged and rippled under a mirror coat. There was not one fleck of white to mark him. He was trotting around his paddock when she appeared, and he gave her a questioning stare, but did not offer to come to her; and Julie did not invite him over, even though she had a pocketful of sugar cubes.

He moved with the grace of a floating cloud; for all his weight, she could not feel or hear his hooves touch the ground. It is not often that a horse who stands over 16.2 demonstrates the lightness and agility of his smaller relatives. Julie watched him for three or four minutes. It was easy to see why he had piled up such a stupefying track record, and she was delighted with him as a mate for Bonnie. He was a superb animal, certainly well up in the top layers of horsedom's royalty.

"I bet I could feed you and you'd be as nice as a lamb," she said. But she hopped down and headed for the van. As she went, she caught a glimpse of a tall man in the doorway of the barren-mare barn where Bonnie was being boarded; he vanished immediately, but she was sure it was Robert Lenkes, and that he had been watching her the whole time.

"Suspicious, aren't you?" she murmured. "And if you're so darned busy, how can you take time to spy on *me?*" She sniffed. "As if a Deepwater girl would . . . would poison your stud or something!"

She got into the van. They drove down to the office beside

the big double gate. The guard appeared and said to the driver, "Inspector Vickel."

"What?" asked Julie's companion, startled.

"Inspector Vickel," he repeated sharply. He sounded as though he were irritably identifying himself as an official of Scotland Yard. Then Julie giggled. "He wants to 'inspect your vehicle,' Jack."

"D'you think I'm kidnapping a horse?" asked the driver blankly.

"Rules. Inspector Vickel."

"Okay, Inspector," said Jack, and got out to open the rear door. Julie went around too and collected Nana, to ride in the front with her. As she settled the pup on her lap, and it wriggled and tried to wash her face, she glanced back at Greyhill. Jack was signing out.

"It's clean, and pretty, and it's efficient, that's for sure," Julie said softly, "but there's something funny about the atmosphere of this farm. I haven't the least idea what it is. Still . . . you know what, little beagle? I don't think I *like* it!"

Chapter VI

February was cold in Kentucky that year, but the first of March brought an unexpectedly warm breeze, and horses began to stamp impatiently in their stalls and sniff the air that wafted in with the scent of sunlight laced through it. Julie and Monty had their hands full, but when Sunday came and he insisted that she take the day off to relax, she agreed readily. "I'm going to visit Bonnie," she said.

"I talked to Lenkes, Greyhill's manager, on the phone only yesterday," Monty said. "She's fine, but I gather they don't encourage casual visitors."

"I'm not casual," said Julie stubbornly, "I'm Bonnie's mother!"

"Yes. Hmm. Well. I suppose you have a moral right to visit her, if you don't give them any trouble."

"What kind of trouble would I give them? You sound like that Lenkes character. Do I give you so much trouble?"

"None whatever, if you don't count Nana eating my slipper yesterday morning under the impression that it was an oatmeal cookie."

"Well, then. All they have to do is open the gate and close it; I'll take it from there. I won't even ask for directions. I think I can remember the way to the stupid barn, even if it was one entire whole *month* ago that I was there," she said tartly.

"Okay, go visit her. I imagine that seeing you will perk her up, anyway. You've never been separated for this long before." Monty passed the teapot. "Bonnie thinks the sun shines only on you, and sometimes I think the reverse is true, too."

Julie worked that one out silently, and then said, "That's not true! I adore Nana, and the Cottabus, and Mr. T, and Dad, and Stash." She poured tea, and grinned at her cup. "You aren't so bad, either, young Everett, till you start bossing me for my own good."

"I never boss you."

"You constantly boss me."

"Well, I am your boss."

"Not in private life."

"I promised your father I'd watch out for you."

"Like a hen over a five-minute-old chick."

"I do not!"

"I know," said Julie placidly, buttering her fourth slice of toast. "I'm kidding. I love to see you turn that funny shade of chestnut."

"Julie," he said plaintively, "will you never be serious with me?"

She regarded him steadily for what seemed to Monty a very long time indeed. Then she said, "Someday," and went on eating.

Someday seemed to him a great stretch of time in the future. He coughed and cleared his throat and opened his mouth, and Dan Gibson came in to breakfast, and Monty went dumb again. Shortly thereafter, Nana came waddling into the kitchen with his other slipper, rather frayed, hanging from the corner of her mouth.

"Congratulations," he said to her moodily. "You've killed the pair of them."

"She knew you wouldn't be using just one," said Julie. She flung on her jacket and whistled to the pup. "We're off to see Bonnie. Expect us for dinner."

"Give her my best," said Monty and Dan in unison.

"Right. Bye." She went out to her car and opened the door for Nana, who pounced in happily. They sped away through the cool and pleasant morning.

At the gate of Greyhill Stud she got out and signed in for the man she would always think of as Inspector Vickel, super sleuth of Scotland Yard. That gentleman was evidently troubled in his mind.

"Does Mr. Lenkes know you're coming?"

"I'm just going to visit my horse, Sunbonnet. I didn't call."

"Does Mr. Grey know you're coming?"

"I doubt it, unless he's a mind reader."

"No, he's the owner. How about——"

"No person knows I am expected," said Julie. "That is, I'm not expected at all, obviously, if nobody knew . . . I mean, you can't expect a visitor that you don't know is coming, can you?"

"What?" said Inspector Vickel, perplexed.

"I am the owner of Sunbonnet, a four-year-old filly who is visiting Bothwell, whom you probably know," Julie explained in a meek voice. "I haven't seen Sunbonnet for a month. She has a bad leg, in which the left-upper sesamoid bone was broken, and I'm anxious to see that it's being treated properly. Do you know Mr. Tolkov?"

"No," said the inspector, completely at sea.

"He is a very rich millionaire. I work for him. I own Sunbonnet. Sunbonnet was Three-Year-Old Filly of the Year. She broke her leg. I decided—"

"All right, all right," said the inspector, throwing up his hands. "Go on up! We only got a skeleton crew on today, it's Sunday, but I guess you know the way."

"I do. Thank you," said Julie demurely. She drove on, waving cheerfully at him. "Inspector Vickel is a dear man," she told Nana, "but he gets confused easily."

She parked beside the barren-mare barn and got out with the beagle. A groom or exercise boy scowled at her briefly, but said nothing and went down the hill. She shrugged and went into the big barn.

Bonnie was in her stall; the bay filly looked as if someone had just brushed her, for even in the relative gloom of the barn her coat shone with its characteristic mahogany glints. Julie slipped through the half-door and embraced her darling, who whickered and nudged the girl with her nose, saying hello. A wave of pure joy went over Julie at the reunion. Even she had not realized how very deeply she had missed her horse.

They talked in their quiet, special fashion for long minutes. Then Julie gave Bonnie an apple and inspected her minutely. She was standing comfortably on all four legs, and she seemd to be at her prime weight. She hadn't wasted away with loneliness, then. Probably the stable hands had made a pet of her, for she was in glorious condition.

"You knew I wasn't gone for good, didn't you?" she asked Bonnie. The horse threw up her head. "I was certain you'd trust me to come back. Well, I wasn't really. I was scared you'd fret. Abandoned in a strange place . . . but you look wonderful!" She gave her a sugar lump. "I was worried myself, I wasn't too sure about this place—but you're fine, and that's all that matters. Wait a minute, I'll find Nana and bring her in," said Julie, realizing for the first time that the beagle had not followed her.

Bonnie put her head over the stall door and watched Julie run down the aisle.

Nana was frolicking in the adjacent pasture, leaping up in small puppy-bounces after invisible butterflies. Julie was about to summon her when a large brown rabbit shot out of the grass where it had been lying low, and dashed away toward the east, with Nana in full pursuit.

"Oh, you *beagle!*" said Julie, after a series of whistles and calls had not had the least effect. Putting her head back into the barn, she threw her filly a brief, apologetic farewell, and ran in the direction Nana had gone. "To think I ever claimed that you looked responsible!" she said under her breath, as a distant flurry of barking rose from over the next hill.

She had run almost a hundred yards before she remembered that Nana had never yet barked. Possibly the pup had found a friend in her wild chase. But when Julie crested the hill, there was Nana, all alone, scurrying along at her best gait and barking her fat little head off.

"It must be the first time you ever had anything to talk about," said Julie angrily, and, lifting her voice, "Nana, come back here!" Nana never even looked over her shoulder, but plunged into the fringes of a sprawling woodland. "At least I know you can bark, even if I had to run half a mile to find out," growled Julie, setting off down the hill. A rabbit bounded away from her feet, likely the same rabbit that Nana thought she was trailing.

"Your obedience training has been sadly neglected," Julie grumbled to the absent beagle as she jumped a creek and went into the chilly, dark woods. For answer, a single yap reached her ears, sounding far off and shrill.

In a few minutes Julie came out of the trees and saw straight ahead and perhaps three hundred yards away a neat little frame house, painted white, with a small two-horse-sized barn and a fenced pasture beyond. A road wound past the place and vanished between two small hills to the south. A man was working in the small yard.

"Maybe he's seen Nana," said Julie to herself, and marched forward to ask him. He must be affiliated with Greyhill Stud in some way, for this, she was certain, was still Greyhill land. Well, perhaps he'd be more jovial than Robert Lenkes and Inspector Vickel. She hoped so. She was a long way from the barn that was supposed to have been her only destination. . . .

"Hi!" she said brightly, pausing beside his front gate.

He straightened from his chore, which was at the moment the weeding of what would be a flowerbed in season. He was a short, sinewy man of middle age, tanned to a shade of cocoa by what must have been a lifetime out-of-doors. Bright green eyes flashed in the weathered face, and his smile was radiant, as though Julie had been his long-lost daughter. When he spoke, his voice was soft but carrying, and his speech was quick.

"Ah, is it yourself, young lady? It is. Come in, don't mind the gate. I didn't know it was closed. A gate should stand open for friends and potential friends alike. Would you like a cup of buttermilk? I broke the last glass only a few days ago—in January sometime—but the buttermilk's fresh. You don't mind it in a cup? I thought you wouldn't. Perhaps a cookie?"

"I'm trespassing after my beagle," Julie said as he paused, evidently for breath.

"I heard a strange bark. That will be your canine buddy. Know every bark and howl on Greyhill, and that was a stranger. Come in. You *do* like buttermilk?"

"Yes," said Julie quickly. He was a character, and a pleasant one too if she was any judge. "Are you Irish?" she couldn't help asking.

"Not that I know of," he said, coming to open the gate. "Were you looking for an Irishman as well as a beagle?"

"No, you sounded sort of Irish."

"That was the phrase 'is it yourself?' I usually start off that way. If a person says 'No,' then I kind of back away, because he doesn't want to let out the secret of who he really is. A good person always admits to being himself. Or herself. As in your case. You didn't need to speak, you know—I could tell it was you."

"Do you know me?"

"I do now, don't I?" he said reasonably. If the tumble and roll of words had come out of anyone else, Julie might almost have thought he was a little odd in the head; but somehow they fitted this brown man, who looked remarkably like a grown-up pixie. Or leprechaun. A faint gleam of mischief shone in the green eyes, she imagined.

"I'm Julie Jefferson."

"Oho! Owner of Sunbonnet, Three-Year-Old Filly of the Year, Handicap Filly of the Year, won all ten races she ran but was technically disqualified once and broke her leg in the last. Lip number"—he closed his eyes for an instant, thinking—"677820. Bought at the Fasig-Tipton for four hundred thousand dollars. Know her well. You're the brave girl that bought her out of a river when she'd been stolen by . . . Well, but you know all that."

"So do you," said Julie, astounded.

"My profession. Horses. Thoroughbreds. Though I take an interest in the Belgian, the Clydesdale, the Percheron too. Grand giants of the earth! I have a pal who's a Percheron. Weighs one ton, even. To the ounce. One vast ton. Incredible! Disposition like a kitten. Introduce you someday." He snapped his fingers. "Sorry, forgot. I'm Carl Larrikin. Call me Pop. Everyone does. Everyone except the boss, Nicholas Grey. Thinks it's undignified, I guess. How about that buttermilk?"

"I really must find my beagle."

"Plenty of time. It'll be hunting out there, and sooner or later Delia will find it."

"Delia?"

"My little hound. She hunts those woods. Just for fun, never catches anything. All the woods and pastures from here to Versailles are her personal domain, if you ask Delia. She'll team up with strangers and bring 'em here for lunch two or three times a week. She'll find your beagle. Come in, get warm, drink your buttermilk. Good for what ails you, if anything does. Are you ailing?"

"Not a bit," said Julie, and could not help laughing. He beamed.

"You looked a bit harried at first. I wondered."

"It's just that Nana is very young, and she's never been off her own territory before."

"Nana. Name's familiar—yes, the nurse-dog in *Peter Pan!*"

"Yes. I called her that because I thought she looked responsible. I was somewhat misled," said Julie, walking down the flagstone path beside him. "You work for Mr. Grey, then?"

"Stud groom. I'm Bothwell's handler. Have you met Bothwell?"

"I was only allowed to look at him."

"Yes," he said, and, surprisingly, was quiet for a moment. "I'll introduce you myself," he said as they went into the tiny, well-kept bungalow. "You'll like Bothwell. He is a lot of horse."

"He's magnificent."

Pop looked at her with admiration. "I knew that Julie Jefferson would be real horse folks," he said. "The record speaks for you. What you did for Sunbonnet! Fantastic. Take a chair. Buttermilk coming up. Cookies? Fresh this morning." If his voice had not been so gentle, the short sentences would have been jerky and perhaps rasping to the nerves; but they all flowed along like the chuckling soft purl of a trout brook. "I'm not a bad baker, but a terrible cook. I once burned the water I was heating for tea. Not many people can burn water. Here." He set a huge plate of sugar cookies on the table next to her, which also held a radio, seven books, a statuette of a racehorse, and a pile of papers weighted down with an old pair of French cut-back blinkers. Somehow it didn't look cluttered at all.

"Everything's so *neat*," Julie said.

"A bachelor has to be neat, or he'll find himself drowned one morning in his own tack. I found that out the hard way: walked into my room one day and fell over a saddle into a sea of dirty dishes. Taught me a lesson. When I came out of the hospital . . ."

Julie whooped with laughter. He gazed at her with mild reproach. "Fact! Snapped my collarbone. I realized I'd actually been piling dishes on the floor to keep from having to wash 'em. Reformed. More fun this way, anyhow—find anything in two ticks. Ask me for something. Dickens, now: *Pickwick Papers*. Second shelf from the top to your left, spang in the center. No pawing through heaps of trash to discover it, see?" He sipped his buttermilk. "Bless the man who invented this glorious brew," he said quietly. "You don't talk a whole lot, do you, Miss Jefferson?"

"Please call me 'Julie.' Yes, I do. Too much, usually."

"Aha. But you find it difficult to get a word in. Flaw in my character. Talk-talk-talk. Why I never married, I suppose. Poor girl never caught the chance to say yes. Assumed she wouldn't, told her good-bye for half an hour or so, ran out of breath, walked mournfully away. She's likely still there, practicing up to say yes in case I ever come back. 'Course, that was before World War II, and she may have got tired of waiting by now. Tell you the trick," said Pop, closing one eye and looking like a man about to tell someone the combination to his safe. "First, clear your throat. Then put on an expression of intense excitement. Hop up and down on one foot. Wave your hands in the air. Grab me by the shirt and shake me hard. Then bellow. You'll get my attention every time."

She smiled at the small man. "You don't fool me," she said comfortably.

He cocked his head and eyed her. "No, I don't. Testing, my dear, testing. Too many folks today think that if you're the least mite different from everyone else, you're strange— a real kook, I believe the expression goes? They haven't been taught that a man—or a woman, mind you, especially a pretty girl—doesn't have to fit the standard pattern in order to be all wool and a yard wide. That's an old-fashioned description. Probably before your time. It means first-rate. Top-notch. Okay. Or better than okay." He slapped his knee. "I knew Julie Jefferson would see through the surface! Has to be a lot of depth in a girl who buys a beat-up and dying filly out of a river, fights criminals to save her, lays her life on the line even, and restores a noble animal to its birthright. Shouldn't even have tested you."

"I didn't mind."

"That's good! Well, I *am* different, you know. Sometimes friends tell me I was invented by Charles Dickens. Ridiculous! I was invented by myself. I enjoy me. Do you enjoy yourself? I bet you do. I think it's a pleasure for you to live in Julie Jefferson's skin, think her thoughts, do her brave deeds. . . ."

"I never do any brave deeds," the girl objected.

"You just don't realize how brave they are. Brave deeds are simply what you *do*, what you *feel* like doing. When you fought Alex Homer, you never sat down afterwards and said, 'That was bold and daring of me!' And yet it was."

Pop Larrikin seemed to know everything that had ever happened to her. Julie said, "Oh, no, I was scared all the way through! I almost fainted when I did that."

"But every soul who ever did a brave thing was scared at the time!" he said, refilling her cup. "That isn't what makes bravery. Bravery's doing what has to be done while your bones are shaking to splinters inside you. How'd we get onto bravery? I was talking about doing your own thing, as they say. So long as you don't hurt other people, or yourself, why,

I think you can be, and do, most anything. And others shouldn't gape and giggle at you for doing it. That's what I meant by 'testing.' I'm me; when I meet someone that looks promising, like a real true friend in the making, I simply intensify me. Talk faster than usual. Overwhelm 'em. See what happens. If they roll with the punches, great. If they back off, peer around for a handy exit, well, the poor creatures must go and find other chums who won't startle 'em by being different. That's all." He took a deep breath. "Larrikin's Law: be yourself. And don't point and snicker when other members of the splendid, silly human race aren't afraid to be *them*selves."

Julie realized that she had never met anyone she had liked so much on such short acquaintance. She thought a moment, and told him so. He wriggled with embarrassment and said, much slower than usual, "I have someone else I'd like you to meet. And many thanks for the compliment, Miss Jefferson."

"Please call me 'Julie,' Pop."

"Right. Julie, while we're waiting for Nana to appear, no doubt all splattered with burrs and painted with mud, I'd like you to come outside and meet an old friend of mine. I believe that you'll like him. I believe you have the sense and the heart to really like him." He bounced to his feet, his vivid green eyes snapping. "Come along, Julie, come along! We mustn't keep a friend waiting!"

They went out into the cool and spring-smelling sunlight.

Chapter VII

"We're going to meet a horse, aren't we?" asked Julie.

Pop gave her a surprised blink. "How'd you guess? It might have been a hound. Or even a person!"

"A hound would be out with Delia. A person would have been invited in to have cookies with us."

"Hmm. Why not a wombat? Some of my best friends, for all you know, may be wombats."

"I felt sure it would be a horse," said Julie.

"Well, it is. Though if he wanted to come in and have cookies . . ."

"You'd bring him in. I know."

They approached the barn. As Julie had noticed, it was about the proper size for two horses; and sure enough, there were two stalls in it, smelling of good clean straw and fine clean horse. In the nearest of these stood a horse.

Julie caught her breath. "Oh, Pop," she whispered, "he's absolutely beautiful!"

And he was. A chestnut stallion of average size—Pop told her afterwards that he stood sixteen hands—his coat was the color of endlessly polished cordovan. His finely chiseled head was thrust out over the half-door toward the visitors, the wide-set eyes staring at them expectantly. He had delicately flared nostrils and a gently tapered muzzle accented by a tiny snip of white.

"May I pet him?"

"Certainly. He's very good-natured, even playful sometimes. Mildest-mannered stallion I ever knew."

Julie moved forward, and Pop opened the door. She rubbed the horse's jaw and smoothed her hand down over the long cheeks. "You beauty," she breathed. The look on his face would not let her take her eyes away from his head for a long minute. He was proud, assured, gentle; wise and alert and friendly; but more than these, he had the expression, often quoted but rarely seen, so frequently attributed to the thor-

oughbred by writers of the turf—the look of eagles. He, like
Bothwell himself, though in a more sympathetic fashion, was
plainly of the horse nobility.

He did not move to come out of the open stall. She stepped
back to take him all in. His slim forelegs ended in a perfectly
matched pair of neat white socks to his ankles. Julie was trying to put her admiration into words when she was caught in
mid-sentence. She had seen that he had a withered, twisted
hind leg.

"Oh!" she gasped. "Oh, you poor dear. . . ."

"He's not poor, and he doesn't need sympathy," said Pop's
voice behind her. "He may look it, but he isn't a poor thing.
He stands tall in his world, and asks for friendship but not
for pity."

She glanced up at his face again. "Yes, you're right. But
oh, my, how terrible for him!"

"It was. It surely was. He would have been one of the
great ones. Do you want to lead him out to pasture? Just
take his mane easily and don't pull. He'll follow."

Julie twined her fingers into the lower strands of the stallion's heavy mane. He stepped out beside her, being courteous
and thoughtful, it seemed to her, about where he placed his
feet. They walked out into the morning together. Pop led the
way, and the fine, maimed animal trod slowly with Julie toward the fenced grazing land.

"Pop, he's a gentleman," said the girl with deep admiration.

"Exactly. We don't teach good manners to racehorses in
the common run of things, you know that; but Tweedy here
was born a gent. I've never known him to do a mean deed.
There isn't a fleck of meanness in his whole body. Even after
what happened to him—tell you about that later. No need to
talk about him to his face," said Pop, precisely as though the
horse understood every word. "Here we are. You can let him
go in now."

The crippled stallion walked deliberately into the pasture
and turned his head to look at her. "You're beautiful," said
Julie with her whole heart in the words. Satisfied, the beast
walked a little farther and began to nibble the graze.

"He eats like a king in his stall," Pop said. "However! He
likes to pretend that wintered stuff is edible, and I let him.
Shall we go see what's for lunch?"

"Won't he be lonesome?"

"No. He knows I won't be away long. He always knows when it's Sunday, and I'll be here all day."

She gave the stallion a lingering last observation, and turned to the house. "I musn't impose on your hospitality. . . ."

"What, lunch? Far nicer to eat with a friend than chew a lonely apple while I weed the yard. Make sense? Does. You can help cook. There's ham and cabbage needs a touch of warming, that's all. I live simply. But there might be ice cream for dessert. If Delia didn't eat the last of it."

"Oh, Nana! I forgot my puppy," said Julie, aghast. "If she gets near a road, she's not used to cars. . . ."

"Delia's a born nursemaid. She won't let her be hurt. Hark!" said Pop suddenly. "Isn't that baying I hear?"

"It must be Delia. Nana only learned to bark today, and as for baying . . ."

"That's Delia and a very young dog," said Pop. "Definitely a pup's bay. Hear it? A touch soprano. That'll be your Nana. Delia's teaching her how to hunt without catching a thing. Invaluable trick. Keeps a dog happy for hours. They'll be in, don't fret. Come and have lunch."

So she did. In half an hour they sat down to a delicious meal that Pop dismissed as "leftovers" but which was about three times the amount that Julie customarily ate in the middle of the day. She felt quite bulgy as she leaned back and sighed that she couldn't finish her ice cream.

"No worry to that. Delia will polish it off as if it were a knucklebone. Now. You want to hear about Tweedy?"

"I do," she told him fervently. "He's so lovely, and it's so sad about his leg."

"No pity, mind! He's his own horse, Julie."

"Yes, I understand. Tell me."

Pop Larrikin aided her to an ancient, comfortable couch. "Stretch out, and I'll tell you his story. As best I can. Never told it before. Don't know whether I'll do it justice. Anyway!" he said, sitting down in his enormous easy chair and beginning to stuff tobacco into an old briar pipe. "Mind smoke? It's my only vice. Besides reading. Ah! Where should I begin?"

"At the beginning," said Julie, feeling logical.

"Excellent advice, old friend." Pop nodded. And she was beginning to consider that they were, indeed, old friends already. He puffed out a fragrant cloud of pipe smoke and thought a moment. When he began to speak, the brief sentences and exclamations were all but gone, and he talked in his soft voice as though he were reading a story from an old and much-loved volume of tales.

"His proper name is Scotch Tweed, by Whole Cloth out of Skye Lassie. Tweedy's his stable name, you understand. He was always something special; from the day of his birth he was special. His bloodlines were good, though not as fine as your Sunbonnet's. But from the instant when I saw him take his first awkward, wobbling steps, and recognized the basic gracefulness that was waiting inside that long-legged little frame, I knew that Tweedy was an exceptional horse—a unique horse.

"You can't explain that feeling. I think it comes from a lifetime of dealing with horses. There's nothing queer about it; it isn't extrasensory perception or anything like that. It's all your life's knowledge of horses working away under the surface of your brains and telling you that this is true and right: this horse is going to be a world-beater.

"I was with him all his life—I ought to say, I have been with him all his life, because we're still together, as you saw. I rubbed his coat with fresh straw when he was born. I put his first baby halter on him when he was six days old. I watched him at play with Skye Lassie, and with the other fillies and colts. When it was time, I took him from Skye Lassie and turned him into a weanling. The owners of the farm where I was head groom (never mind its name, it makes me angry just to say it out loud) had decided they wouldn't send Tweedy to the yearling sales, but would keep him and race him as they did with their best horses. So naturally he grew into a hardy, independent, sunburned young fellow, which was really better for him than being fattened up for the auctions.

"Independent, yes, but even then always the gentleman. Rugged, but with a sweet disposition, more like that of a pampered old mare than of a stallion."

Pop relit his briar thoughtfully, searching for words, for the right approach to the story. Julie kept silent, enthralled.

"I broke him as carefully as I'd ever broken a thoroughbred in my life. More so, I think. It was almost five months from the day I put a bit into his soft mouth for the first time to the day when I let Girty ride him through his first breeze."

"Is that Reg Girty?" she couldn't help asking.

"Yes, do you know him?"

"He kept me from riding Bonnie in the Forget-Me-Not last year," said Julie, "but he was right. He's a good jockey."

"I never let any but the best climb onto Tweedy's saddle."

"Go on, please!"

"Well, when he'd learned to work with other horses, I schooled him myself. He was a miracle in the gate, just as though he knew what it was all about. And in his workouts at the track, where I took him as a two-year-old, he showed absolutely blazing speed. I tell you, those works were fantastic! I knew I'd been right. He was going to make his name famous. He'd be up there with Citation and Whirlaway and Old Bones. Maybe even Big Red himself—that was Man o' War, you know.

"I was head groom by choice, but I had my trainer's license too, and the owners wanted me to see him well into his career, because they knew horses, and they could see how close Tweedy and I were, and how obediently he'd go through his proper paces for me. So that's how I came to be at the track with him.

"Then, while he was being readied for his first race, he was up to be okayed out of the gate. There were three others up that day as well, so four youngsters went out there to break out of the gate for the starter and earn their gate cards, which would tell the world that they were expert enough at leaving the post to be allowed to compete in actual races."

Pop Larrikin paused and blew his nose ferociously. Julie thought there were unshed tears in the bright green eyes. But he continued placidly with his story, no tension in his voice to warn her that the terrible part was coming.

"I was leaning on the rail watching. The exercise boy eased my bright little colt into the number-three stall of the gate. Two others stood quietly on his left, one on his right. The bells rang, the doors flew open in front of the colts—in front of three of them."

"Three?" Julie gasped, sitting up straight on the old couch.

"Yes. Three flashes of color went streaking all blurred down the track. The fourth was my great, gallant Scotch Tweed.

"He'd been poised and ready for his usual flight. Then the bells clanged out and he knew he had to spring from the gate —oh, the countless times he'd done it before—practicing, perfecting his timing; he knew what he had to do, and he trusted those bells, as I'd taught him to. They meant he was ready to get away fast.

"So when they rang, he made his tremendous thrusting shove with his hindquarters; and then there must have been terrible searing pain all through him as his chest hit the door that was *still closed*. It had jammed in front of him.

"He fell twisted, his front legs thrashing wildly, his right hind leg crumpled beneath him. When he fell, it was as though a shattering explosive force had been detonated in a small box. Blood was spurting, and pieces of hair and hide were left inside the gate. It was horrible. I was running toward him almost as it happened, trying to stop the accident right there, to turn it around, take it back through time and force it *not* to happen. That sounds crazy, but it's how I felt. Then I came to myself, and I was right there, and all I could think of was how to help him, my fine chestnut colt."

Julie was weeping, but she did not know it. Her heart was out on that long-ago track with Tweedy.

"The men who were in range of the awful noise—assistant starters, the exercise boy, one or two other fellows—came right behind me. We swarmed over the fighting animal, and the boy fell down within range of those flailing hooves and had to be hauled out of harm's way instantly. We set to freeing Tweedy as fast as we could.

"It just about didn't matter by then. He knew that he couldn't get up, couldn't run down the lane as I'd taught him to do, not now. How do we know what a horse knows? Maybe he knew he wasn't ever going to run again. He stopped fighting, because there was nothing left for him to fight with.

"We dragged him from under the gate, for it was easier to move the colt than the gate, and stood there watching that lovely chestnut beast lying on the track, his coat black with sweat and stained with his blood, his right hind leg skewed around at a terribly unnatural angle to his body. Then the vet was there."

Pop lit his pipe again. His hands were the least bit shaky. Living that day over again was hard. "Tranquilizers," he said jerkily, "painkillers, everything possible. Somehow we got him up, there were a dozen of us then, and loaded him into the horse ambulance.

"They took X-rays. The bone was crushed. It made you

sick to look at the X-rays, let alone the leg. I admit that I was moving in a fog. I couldn't believe it had happened, but I knew that it had. I don't know whether I hoped or not. I don't remember what I felt.

"The vet studied the X-rays a long time, and said it was hopeless. I said it couldn't be. He said it was. I think I came near punching him in the jaw for that. It was not hopeless. I kept saying that to everyone.

"Again we got the poor fellow into the ambulance and drove him more than a hundred and fifty miles, to the big animal clinic of Strandhill University. There are good horse centers like it in the University of Pennsylvania's New Bolton Center and at Cornell too, but we were closest to Strandhill. Some of the finest specialists in the country were waiting there, to see if they could shed some light in the darkness that was looming up as my brave young colt's future. Dr. Carleton, head of the Orthopedic Department, and the foremost equine bone specialist in the United States—perhaps in the world—said that there was a chance to save him if the owners, my bosses, wanted to use him for breeding purposes. But he also said that he'd never walk normally again; and as for running, that was not in the cards for Tweedy, not ever again, not possibly."

Pop handed Julie a dish of peppermints. "Takes away that full feeling, my dear; I see your eyes are bulging."

"I'm just trying not to cry," said Julie, whose face was moist with tears. She ate a peppermint. "Go on, Pop."

"Well, Tweedy's owners turned out to be a greedy, heartless bunch of good-for-nothing money-grabbing wretches if I ever saw one, and they preferred to declare the colt a total loss and have him destroyed."

"Oh!" Julie exclaimed, indignant and scowling.

"They expected to collect a pretty tidy sum in insurance money, you see. However, the insurance company, which was faced with a large payoff, balked. Since Dr. Carleton said the colt could possibly be saved, they weren't willing to approve of Tweedy's being put down."

"Yay!" cried Julie. "Hooray for them."

"That's well said. They were interested in the money end of it, of course, but they saved Tweedy's life by it. The owners said that they weren't going to spend the sum it would take to fix him up properly, neither at Strandhill nor especially at the private centers, which naturally cost even more.

They said he was well-bred, but not superlatively bred, and that no matter how great I claimed he would have been, that was only my belief in the colt as an individual, and not strictly a product of his breeding. So they said No. They expected to see no return on their money if they did such a blame fool thing, not for years and maybe not ever, and No, they washed their hands of him, never wanted to see him again, or me—I'd been fairly bitter in talking to them, you can imagine, and I'd called the big boss several plain-spoken nasty names—and, in short, they wouldn't pay a dollar for any work on the colt and that was that. They wrote him off as a total loss. And I never went near them again, but had a pal go and collect my gear and send it on to me. Come to think of it, they still owe me three weeks' wages. I don't mind. I don't want their money.

"Well, the insurance men, who were very decent people in addition to being good businessmen, were quite willing to pay for the necessary operations, lodging, and care that Tweedy would need to restore him to health if possible. Otherwise, they'd have had to part with a great deal higher sum of money for the mortality claim.

"You understand all this technical rigmarole so far, Julie?"

She nodded. Pop continued. "So, as the cheapest and the more humane choice, the insurance company footed Tweedy's bills at Strandhill University. I stuck with the colt through the whole thing. Couldn't have done otherwise. After a while it was obvious that he was going to live—he has a fine constitution, but I'll always believe that it was his tremendous heart that pulled him through—and then, a long time later, that he would be able to walk.

"Naturally, the insurance company isn't in the stud-farm business, and they had to sell him. I reckoned up my resources . . . luckily, I've always lived rather plainly, and I had some money, if not anywhere near the amount that they'd spent on his recovery. . . . To make a long story bearable, I bought the colt from them.

"A year or two before that, Nicholas Grey had asked me to come to work as his stud groom. Now I took him up on the offer. I knew there was this little house, with the barn and pasture, and I could have Scotch Tweed with me here.

"That was what mattered to me. He'd been so patient, such a thorough gentleman, if we can overwork that word once more, and I'd loved him for so long, that by now he was what mattered to me, and very little else did.

"Mind, Julie, the world isn't one horse for me. I'm fond of Bothwell and half a dozen other fine big stallions on this farm. I enjoy my work. I like all four seasons, and storms and fine sunny days and buttermilk—would you like some? —and Delia and, oh, more sidekicks and friends than I ever bothered to count. But Tweedy, well, he's the basic breath of my life. And I believe that's how he feels about me."

"Like Bonnie and me," said Julie.

"Right. So I left the track for good, brought Tweedy to this house, and settled in. The situation was ideal, because there's a river over east there where I could swim him and strengthen the injured leg. I started my own vegetable garden out back, and I couldn't ask for a better roosting place.

"It was half a dozen years ago that we came here, Tweedy and I. He's eight now. He may have twenty years or more left. He's happy, healthy, and his leg doesn't bother him in the slightest.

"There's only one thing that saddens me a little. . . . Listen!" said Pop, breaking off and cupping one ear. "Don't I hear a bark at the door?"

"I didn't hear it." Julie was anxious to know what saddened him.

"I'm sure that was Delia's open-up woof." He got out of his chair and darted to the front door like a boy of twelve. "Ah, here you are, then, late for lunch," he said mock-severely. "And who's your round little pal with the muck on her ears?"

Julie flew to the door to see for herself.

Chapter VIII

It was Nana, trailing behind a little brown-and-white hound with a downcast air, and it would have been impossible to determine which of them had collected more burrs, more muck, or more thorns in the coat. They marched in over the spotless rug.

"Oh, Nana, no! You're filthy!" Julie made as though to eject her puppy, but Pop put a hand on her arm and shook his head.

"No, she's a friend of Delia's, and Delia lives here. They have a perfect right to track in mud. They can't wipe their feet, at least with any amount of success. Never get mad at an animal because it isn't a human being. I can clean up mud easier than I could explain to Delia and her guest why they weren't welcome."

Nana, as exhausted as only a puppy can look, collapsed at her mistress's feet and rolled up one eyeball in a gaze of affection and a plea for help.

"Water first," said Pop, setting down a large bowl. Nana found the energy to waddle over and lap up a bit, after which Delia took her turn. "Now meat," said Pop, dishing that out. Julie noticed that there was a plateful for each dog. Pop Larrikin was a truly kind man. Even her father's two retrievers ate from one platter. "And to top it off, ice cream," said Pop, getting it from the refrigerator. "But eat your meat first. Then we'll tidy you. What a time you must have had! Look like a pair of walking swamps."

"I'm taking up half your day," said Julie, apologetic.

"You're filling half my day with pleasure."

"Oh. I'm glad. That's how I feel."

He was still a marvelous surprise to her, especially after the cold shoulders at Greyhill Farm. And his story was an admirable example of the devotion that a good horse inspires in a good man. Due to Pop Larrikin's diligent care and endless affection, the broken horse Scotch Tweed was

an obviously happy animal. She thought to herself, watching
him feed the dogs, Why, I'd rank Pope with the finest people
I know: Dad, Stash, Mr. T, Leon, Monty. . . . She wondered what it was that saddened him. It would be all right
to ask him, she felt sure, or else he would never have said
anything about it. Probably it was that Tweedy had never
been able to fulfill his destiny as a superb racer.

Pop put down the ice cream, as the pup and the hound
were both finished inhaling their main course, and came back
to sit opposite her again. "Can't I offer you some refresh-
ment, Julie?"

"Oh, gosh, Pop, I won't be able to take anything in the
line of food for days. I'm stuffed up to the chin, honest.
What were you going to tell me? About something making
you sad?"

"That. Yes. I wanted to breed Tweedy, you know, to pass
on his speed, his courage, his marvelous conformation—
his incredible lungs and heart and legs. I wanted a lot of
foals to be born with his unparalleled personality. You
know how you want that for Sunbonnet. Same with me.
But poor Tweedy was cut down before his prime, before he
could establish himself in competition. His bloodlines are
good, as I told you, but don't warrant blind-faith breeding,
it seems. Can't blame folks. I'm the only one who remem-
bers his speed in the workouts. No one wants to breed mares
to him."

"That's awful," said Julie, frowning fiercely at all the
absent people who couldn't see the innate greatness of
Scotch Tweed. "Can't you do *something?*"

He was silent for a long time, longer, it seemed, than the
question called for. Then at last he said, "I've just bought
myself a pretty good mare. Oh, she's no youngster. She's
aging. If she were a chicken, you'd hesitate to make soup
out of her. But she's produced a number of winners at the
track. Yes. Good dam in her day, her produce are superior
horses. I got her at a sale; had my eye on her for several
years. When she's in foal to Tweedy, I'll feel a little better.
But I wish I'd bought her, or one like her, years ago. My
stallion should have established his worth as a stud before
this. And it saddens me. But only a little! I don't go around
blubbering. Neither does he." Pop shook his head once, hard.
"Couple of tough old antiques, we are, Tweedy and I."

"Oh, pooh," said Julie. "That's how Leon talks, and it's pure hot air and horse feathers."

Pop wrinkled his brow. "That'd be Leon Pitt."

"You know everything!" cried the girl, amazed.

"No, no. Only *seem* to. You work for Rollin Tolkov. So does Leon Pitt. Simple. Elementary, I might say, my dear Jefferson."

"Anyway, I think you're proud of being old—I mean, middle-aged—and like to seem older. But you can't. Energy!" said Julie, imitating him. "Bounce! Keep up with men half your age. Tweedy too."

"I've infected you with the ridiculous speech patterns of a constant reader of Dickens," said Pop, twinkling. "Time we cleaned up the dogs, don't you think? Before they go to sleep on those basketballs they call their stomachs."

This took half an hour of intense work with rags, combs, and prying, picking fingers. At last, though, the adventurous beasts were relatively clean and burrless. "Now I have to go," said Julie regretfully. "My car's parked beside the barren-mare barns, and if Mr. Lenkes finds it there, he'll have the police searching for me."

"You aren't exaggerating much," said Pop. "Hate to lose you, Julie, you're almighty fine company. Would be nice if you spoke up oftener, but you'll learn that. Get over your shyness. Will you stop laughing helplessly when I'm being so serious? Younger generation," he grumbled, "no respect. Tell 'em a fact, and they whoop at you. You think about what I said. Work on it. Interrupt people, no matter how backward you feel. Good for the throat, airs it out wonderfully. Sure you won't have a last glass of buttermilk? Okay, then pick up your Nana and trudge back to the main buildings. Find your way? Good. I think that pup's sound asleep. No wonder!"

"She'll sleep all the way home."

"Likely. Next time you come by, drop in again. I'm here every Sunday. And by next week my mare will be here too. Name of Kimberley Gem. I think you'll like her too."

"I'm sure I will. Say good-bye to Tweedy for me. And thanks for all the super hospitality, Pop."

She walked back through the woodland, up the hill, and across the pastures with Nana slumbering in her arms, emitting tiny pup-snores as she dreamed of the pursuit of rabbits. Again there was no one visible near the barns, and after laying Nana tenderly on the passenger seat of her car, Julie went in to say hello-and-bye to Bonnie. Her filly nosed her curiously, as if scenting a strange horse on her jacket. "That's Tweedy," Julie told her. "He's simply a terrific horse! I hope you can meet him someday." She caressed her beloved racer. "I almost wish," she said slowly, thinking of it for the first time, "that you could have your foal by him. I know, Bothwell has a wonderful record, and he's absolutely gorgeous, but Tweedy . . . well, Tweedy is extra, extra special. But I guess that isn't practical. Monty would never dream of allowing it."

She thought further. "Not that Monty's your boss. I am, and when it comes to foals, Mr. T. Honey, I have to think about this. You be good, and eat what they give you, and don't be scared. I'll visit soon again, in spite of all the cool stares I get." She kissed Bonnie on the brow and went to her car.

Inspector Vickel gave her a long, puzzled glare, then waved her on. She drove home at the speed limit, and Nana bounced around all over the seat and never woke up at all till she was carried in and deposited on Julie's bed.

That evening after a skimpy dinner, caused by her immense lunch, Julie took Monty over to the fireplace and set him down firmly. "I have to tell you some things, boss," she said soberly.

"Something wrong?" He'd wondered why she had been so uncharacteristically quiet through the meal.

"I don't know. I don't like the *feel* of Greyhill, Monty. Nobody's friendly, except the stud groom, Bothwell's handler. He's Pop Larrikin, and he's really neat. But everyone else who sees me looks as if he'd like to kick me off the place."

"I told you, they're busy there."

"We're busy here, but when strangers come to see the place, even without appointments, Mr. T has them shown around royally. Greyhill's kind of chilly and . . . downright spooky."

"Haunted by the ghosts of girls who weren't allowed to move in with their fillies," suggested Monty.

"You're so smart. I know that I don't have much to go on, suspecting I-don't-know-what, but my intuition tells me there's something out of kilter at Greyhill. Something downright onimous."

"You mean 'ominous.'" He stretched out his feet to the fire.

"You know I can never get that word right. Okay, then, call it scary. I don't know if they're hiding something criminal, or immoral, or improper, or what, but I *sense* it the minute I drive in the gate and Inspector Vi—I mean, the guard has me sign in, and peers at me as if I was bringing in a horse-eating tiger or a bomb! And Lenkes, the manager, acts suspicious of me, but I'd think that it was just his personality except for this—today I passed a groom, and *he* looked at me really weird, as if I was trespassing."

"Intruding on a busy farm is more like it."

"But what can they have to hide from a girl whose filly is there being readied for breeding?" demanded Julie.

"I have no idea. If that's all you have to go on, I think your suspicions are unjustified."

"It isn't; today Pop said one or two things, as though he was going to tell me something about the owner and about Lenkes, and then sheered off from them. And he was quiet, too, once or twice when it didn't seem to fit with what he was saying."

"Julie, you know that everyone doesn't talk as constantly as you often do. It's natural to pause—"

"It wasn't quite natural when Pop did it. If you met him, you'd see what I mean. Monty, I want you to go to Greyhill Stud with me. Next Sunday. I want you to meet Pop, and Tweedy too, but I specially want you to get the atmosphere of the place at first hand."

"Who's Tweedy?"

She told him about Tweedy and his sad history. "I was sort of wondering, Monty, if we could send one or two of Mr. T's mares to him. Maybe Bandicoot."

Monty laughed. "Whoa! Back up a way. You can't go breeding Mr. T's top mares to an unknown, unproven stallion just because you like his face! That's wild even for you, Julie."

"If you heard Pop tell about his speed, and if you saw him—Tweedy, I mean—why, he has the look of eagles!"

"I wouldn't go behind Mr. T's back to breed a mare to a stud who had the look of cheetahs or baboons or any other flesh-fish-or-fowl. You know better than that." Monty began to be actually irritated with her. "What's got into you, anyway? That farm has rattled your brains, Julie."

"It has, I admit it, but this hasn't got anything to do with Greyhill. Brrr!" she exclaimed, shuddering. "Even the name sounds creepy. But Scotch Tweed is something else. I never liked the look of a horse so much, except for Bonnie, not ever. Think of the way he started out, before he had that awful accident. And Pop is so nice, such a good *horse* man, imagine how wonderful it would be if his faith in Tweedy could be justified! It's grim to see a fine horse growing old without any get, any progeny to carry on his blood!"

"Yes, it is, but we don't know anything about what sort of get he'd have," said Monty, "get" being the word for a stallion's offspring. "The answer is, regretfully, no. N-o, no."

"You are simply the most rigidly inflexible and conventional man in the entire state of Kentucky!" snapped Julie angrily. "And that goes for Ohio, too. You never want to take a single tiny chance at anything different."

"Not with another man's horses, no."

She sizzled audibly for a moment and then calmed down. She got up and stood staring into the flames, leaning on the side of the hearth. "Oh," she said, "oh, it's a drag, but you're right. It would be all wrong to do it. But if Bonnie's foals were all mine, and not half Mr. T's, then I'd breed her to Tweedy without a second thought."

"And I'd try to argue you out of that, too, because the horse has no record; but you'd ignore all my superb advice, and probably get a foal that would go on to win the Triple Crown. Alas, Julie, there isn't a mare available that we could honestly send to him. Unless you want to buy Bandicoot from Deepwater Farm and try *that*."

"Maybe I will," said Julie darkly, "maybe I just will. But first I'll think some more."

"I wasn't quite serious about Bandicoot."

"I was." She took a marshmallow out of a box on the mantel, stuck it on a toasting fork, and held it over the fire till it had browned. Then she offered it to Monty. "Sorry, I do get carried away. But I'm going to help Pop *do* something for that little chestnut horse."

Monty nodded and ate the marshmallow. "I feel sure that you will," he said.

Chapter IX

One week later, Monty and Julie and Nana drove off to visit Bonnie. They intended, too, that their trip should include an hour or so with Pop Larrikin and his stallion, as well as the stud groom's new mare.

Inspector Vickel came out of his office, and when he recognized Julie, a cloud of some unpleasant emotion went over his face that was so obvious that even Monty noticed it.

"Are you here again?"

"Yes," said Julie demurely, "and I've brought the well-known trainer Montgomery Everett of Deepwater Farm with me. We want to visit Sunbonnet."

"Did you check first with Mr. Lenkes?"

"No," said Monty shortly. "Why should we? Our mare is here to be bred."

"Did you check with Mr. Grey?"

"No!" shouted Monty. He was not used to such interrogation.

"Did you check with—"

"Dear Inspector Vickel, nobody knows we're coming. Again." Julie smiled sweetly at him. "I know that you have only a skeleton crew on duty, this being Sunday. I know where the three barren-mare barns are located. I know in which of these resides, temporarily, my own filly, Sunbonnet. I am familiar with the road to that barn. I don't need directions, instructions, or anything except a jolly word of welcome."

"What did you call me?" asked the guard suspiciously.

Julie gulped. "Nothing," she said. The nickname had slipped out.

"Sign in," he grumped at Monty, who climbed out and did so. Then the guard waved them briefly toward the farm. "Don't go nowheres else but your horse's stall, understand?"

"Right on, chief," said Monty between clenched teeth, and drove slowly up the road. "Julie," he said, "I'm sorry.

You were perfectly right. That's borderline rudeness with no excuse for it. And if Lenkes acts the way you say, then : . ."

"He does. I don't imagine such things. He makes you feel just as unwelcome as Inspector Vickel." She showed him the route to the barn, then where to park. She lifted Nana off her lap. "No rabbit-chasing today, little beagle, or Mother will have to buy a leash for you." Nana gazed back at her with innocent, respectful big eyes. Julie set her on the ground, where the dog stood passively waiting orders.

"In here," said Julie, and Monty followed her into the clean, fresh-smelling barn. They greeted Bonnie and fussed over her and admired her condition, which was, as before, immaculate. Monty watched her and thought heavily while Julie fed the filly a carrot and some sugar. "I forgot gumdrops," said Julie, "what with so much worry and all."

"She couldn't be in better shape, and that's really all that should worry us about this place," Monty said. "Still, I agree, I am not bubbling with happiness over the atmosphere. I never saw cleaner stalls or a more well-cared-for horse, though. All I've really seen is a sour guard on the gate."

"But why the warning not to go anywhere else but here? I told him who you are. Why wou'd he think we'd go anywhere else? You'd think they'd want to show off their stock to you." Julie shook her head. "I just don't get it, Monty."

"I don't either. Your intuition's rubbing off on me, though. I don't feel comfortable here. I don't know, maybe it's only the lack of people. They must have a big crew to keep this place so spotless. Where are they? Even on Sunday. And are they *all* distrustful? And why?"

"That's how I've been talking to myself for weeks."

"Julie," said the young man solemnly, "if I ever make light of your opinions again, kick me in the shins."

"Monty," said Julie, "I promise."

They examined Bonnie's left foreleg together. It looked all right, and the filly apparently favored it only slightly in moving around her stall. Then Monty straightened and put his hands on Julie's shoulders to look into her eyes.

"It couldn't have been better if you'd been looking after it yourself all these weeks. Julie, we're being silly. How suspicious and rude the Greyhill staff is doesn't mean a thing to us. What counts is Bonnie, and she's as chipper as ever. So let's quit being sensitive about the atmosphere. If *she's* all right, then nothing else is any of our business. Right?"

Julie squirmed a little. "Weellll," she said finally, "okay."

"Good. Have you spent enough time with her? We mustn't take her out; that would be pushing our pushiness too far."

"Where's Nana? Oh, man," said Julie, "if she's gone baying after another bunny, I'll just die. She was here in the straw only a minute ago. . . ."

"Come on," said Monty, "I hear a faint bark."

"Bye, Bonnie baby," said Julie, hugging her filly quickly. Then they ran out into the rather overcast and grayish morning. The beagle was nowhere to be seen.

"She's found somebody's slipper," said Monty, revolving on one heel and scanning the countryside. "We should have left her in the car."

"But she misses Bonnie so."

"How can you tell?"

"The look in her eyes."

"That is about as preposterous an idea as I've heard all year," said Monty. "Whistle for the brute, we can't have her trespassing. Inspector Vickel would put her in jail."

Julie whistled and called. A muffled bark replied, from the next barn to the west, which was some hundred yards distant.

"Oh, wow, that's one of the other mare barns," said Julie. "We mustn't go in there." She called urgently again. Nana replied in an abstracted tone.

"We have to get her out. Come on," said Monty. "She's liable to stampede some skittish mare." They raced over and into the barn side-by-side.

Nana came to greet them, wagging her entire rear half joyously. "Wicked!" said Julie, snatching her up. Then, just for a moment, she gazed around the barn. There were many mares here, and with some of them stood foals of various sizes. Julie, bewildered, was about to ask Monty what was going on here, when he gripped her arm, his face bleak.

"Out, fast. Before we wind up in deep trouble."

"I don't understand . . ." Then she was rushed bodily to the door of the barn, where they stopped, Julie's mouth open. "But, Monty!"

He moved a few steps out from the place, looking around. And a tall, heavily mustached man came from behind Bonnie's barn and, seeing them, stopped dead. It was the manager, Lenkes.

"Hey!" he bellowed, advancing now and waving his arms

in a definitely threatening manner. "Don't go into that barn!"

"I won't," said Monty in his mildest tone.

"What do you think you're doing here, anyhow?" demanded Lenkes, stopping beside them. Monty was tall, but this man towered over him. "Who are you?"

"This is Miss Jefferson, who owns—"

"I know her. Who are you?"

"Everett, trainer for Deepwater Farm."

"This isn't the barn your filly's housed in. Don't you know that? This is private property."

"We were looking at Bonnie," Julie put in, "and my dog ran outside, so we just followed her so she wouldn't frighten the foals."

"There aren't any foals near here," said Lenkes sharply. "What made you think that?"

"Thought I heard a foal nicker inside there," said Monty.

"You have a tin ear, sonny. That barn's full of our own Greyhill mares, and not a foal among 'em. That's a barren-mare barn."

"Oh. My error. Can we look at them?"

"Sorry," said Lenkes, relaxing a little. "Against the rules. Strangers annoy some of them. Why don't you go look at your own mares at Deepwater, if you want to look at mares?"

"I guess we will," said Monty, and taking Julie by the elbow, firmly steered her to the car. Lenkes stood looking after them until they had closed the door; then he went into the barn.

"Monty," Julie began earnestly.

"Not now. Outside." He drove down to the gate, and, as it was open at the moment, straight on outside the limits of Greyhill, not bothering to glance at the guard on duty there. When they had turned the first corner in the main road, he pulled over and stopped.

"Were you ever right about that place!" he said, and took a deep breath and shook his head violently. "Do you know what it means? What we saw in that barn?"

"It means that Robert Lenkes is a plain out-and-out liar. He said there were nothing but mares in there."

"Did you get a good squint at those foals? This is the eleventh of March—and from the look of them, those aren't even *January* foals. Would you believe November?"

"So?"

"So they must be kept hidden away like that until there

are enough babies of varying sizes to camouflage them. In a couple of months they can be passed off as just Greyhill's usual fine individuals, outstanding among their peers. Right now, though, it's obvious what they are—a barnful of early foals!"

Julie widened her eyes. Of course! No matter how late in the year a foal is born, he is by the laws of the Jockey Club a year old on New Year's Day, even if he's been teetering around on his rickety legs for only a couple of hours. "Then they aren't registered yet," she said.

"That's right. Otherwise, why the secrecy? They'll be registered as foals born this month and next, I'd guess. Greyhill must breed their own mares for late-year foaling, hide them like this, and register their offspring in February, March, and April. It's one gigantic hoax, and—"

"Why would they do that?" asked Julie. She thought she knew, but it was hard for her to recognize the fact that an operation as big, as well-known, and as firmly established as Greyhill Stud would stoop to such a dirty trick.

"Why? To make a stack of money, that's why. No wonder the yearlings from Greyhill are always the biggest and strongest-looking at the August sales! Their 'yearlings' are actually anywhere from eighteen to twenty-one, maybe twenty-two months old. Most of the consigners' horses are from fourteen to eighteen months. That's an edge of as much as eight months in age, and you know the big difference that even two or three months can make in a yearling's price at sale time!"

"Monty," she burst out indignantly, "that's outright brazen cheating!"

"Yes," he agreed, and glanced at her sadly. "I'm afraid your new friend Pop Larrikin is in it too, up to his eyebrows."

"That's a dreadful thing to say. Why should he be in on it?"

"Because with a whole barn full of foals, hidden away from strangers' eyes, but there for any employee to walk in on at any time, the whole scheme has to be known to everyone on the farm; and Pop is a stud groom, and the handler of Bothwell, who must be the sire of a good many of those foals. Even the exercise boys, the guards, the cook, and all must know."

"Not Pop," said Julie without much conviction.

"Nobody's so stupid that he couldn't figure out the reason for all those concealed foals."

"You're right," said Julie miserably.

"And the thing is, what they're doing can't even get them slung into jail. I don't think there's any law of the land that says you can't lie about your age . . . even if you're a colt or a filly. It isn't exactly illegal; it just makes Greyhill's yearlings outstanding individuals by comparison with the other consignments."

"It's just ghastly," said Julie, petting Nana and thinking. "I can hardly believe it, but I know it's true. That's why the place has such a suspicious, belligerent, go-away feel to it. 'Cause that's how they have to act, with that hocus-pocus fraud going on. I wouldn't be surprised if everyone on that farm was a jailbird."

"Well, now, not that bad. I imagine most of them just look the other way and don't figure it's important enough to get worked up over. Probably some of them are actively in on it, and some others get slight bonuses to keep their mouths shut, and others ignore the whole thing. But it's misrepresentation, and it's wrong, and I don't like Bonnie being there, even though I know she's quite safe and Bothwell will make her a good match."

"Yes, I understand how you feel. As if Bonnie might get . . . well, dirty, just from living in the middle of it. It's crazy," Julie admitted, "but I'd almost like to take her home."

"The fraud won't rub off on Bonnie. They do take care of their horses well, and especially high-priced horses belonging to other owners. Mr. T is a pillar of the turf; they'd be extra careful of his horse. But I don't like it. I'm going to do some detective work when we get home, and see what I come up with regarding Greyhill, and Mr. Nicholas Grey."

"You're certain sure Bonnie'll be safe?"

"Yes, honey, this isn't a case of crooks trying to steal her, you know; it's just a sort of slimy get-more-for-a-horse-than-it's-worth deal that we've discovered, thanks to Nana."

"We couldn't be wrong about it? Could it have some other meaning, all those foals that Lenkes says aren't foals?"

"None that I can imagine. Ready to go home?"

Julie fingered her lower lip and thought. Then she drummed her fingers on her blue-jeaned knee, which was a sign of nervous tension that Monty recognized. At last she heaved a sigh and said, "I'm ready. I know she'll be okay.

I know, somehow, that Pop Larrikin is okay, too. I want to stay here and find out everything. But you're right. Let's go home."

Monty put the car in gear and drove away from Greyhill Stud Farm under a lowering and rain-filled cover of dark clouds.

Chapter X

By suppertime Monty had telephoned almost everyone he knew in the racing game, and had arrived precisely at the point from which he'd set out: namely, his own suspicion plus nothing else.

True, there were stories of people being discouraged from visiting Greyhill in wintertime; once or twice a rather puzzled note in someone's voice as he related how Lenkes, or the owner, Nicholas Grey, friendly as you could wish in the autumn, grew distant and cool, downright unfriendly even, as New Year's approached. But plainly no one had ever heard a breath of scandal, or suspected any sort of fraud, connected with the Greyhill Stud.

"Best-kept secret in the business," Monty growled to the fidgeting girl after what she estimated was his umpteenth long-distance call. "It's incredible, Julie, but we must be the only outsiders who've ever stumbled into the barn, ever seen those hidden foals. Yet Greyhill's at least fifteen years old. I remember the phrase 'a Greyhill colt' being used with admiration when I was barely toddling around St. Clair's stable. They've always had the reputation for big, rugged colts and fillies. This early foaling explains that. Why hasn't the explanation ever leaked out?"

"Because they're gangsters, and they threaten their workers," said Julie darkly. "Dead men tell no tales."

"You watch too much television. They aren't gangsters any more than Nana is. They're just cheats. Now, if someone saw a foal or two out in a paddock or meadow with its dam, that would be easy to pass off. 'Yes, she dropped her foal in 320 days, when we were counting on 340—our tough luck, but you can't win 'em all,' and that would be that. I think the barn must be guarded very carefully and that we got into it by a fluke. The gate guard must have phoned all over the place to find Lenkes after he'd had to let us in. Come to think of it, I remember hearing at

91

least two phones ringing while we were with Bonnie—quite a way off, as though they were in different places. Probably there was someone in that barn, too, last, time you were there; and if you'd headed that way, instead of over the hills after Nana, you'd have been stopped."

"Shot down in my very tracks."

"No, snarled at ferociously for a trespasser."

"If they kept a guard at the gate who was a little brighter than Inspector Vickel, he'd have found some pretext to keep us out of Greyhill to begin with," said Julie.

"Right. I'll bet he caught it from Lenkes after we'd gone. I'd almost bet you won't get in again, unless Lenkes himself bird-dogs you around."

"You're convinced that Bonnie's in no danger?"

"Yes. Not the faintest shadow of doubt."

"Then I suppose it would be silly to take her away."

"It would be a clear loss of eighteen thousand dollars."

"And that would be dumb. What do we do, then? Forget it? I don't much like that."

Monty knew how she felt about honesty; it was one of the few things in the world more important to her than Bonnie. He had anticipated the question. "You know, I'm going out to Kandahar Park tomorrow with Cottabus and Millie Maypou. I'll be gone three days. Mr. T is in New York till Thursday. There's no time or chance to do anything now. But when we both come home, I'll huddle with him and make the decision then. I know he won't just let it go. He's too fine a man to wink at chicanery like that."

"And meanwhile . . ."

"You'll sit tight, say nothing, and rest easy because Bonnie is just as safe as she'd be in her Deepwater stall."

"If you say so, boss," Julie assented. She pondered over the pecan pie. Then she said, "But I don't like the aroma of the whole situation one tiny little smidgen!" And that was the last word on the subject that night.

Monty left early with the horses. Julie did her chores, dividing them even with Dan Gibson, and thought until her head began to ache. At last she said to Dan, "I have an errand to run. Can you make do without me for a few hours?"

"Why, sure, Julie; Mickey can fill in for you." He cocked an eyebrow. "Bonnie?"

"Well, in a way. I want to talk to Pop Larrikin."

"Who? Oh, the groom over at Greyhill. Okay, will we see you for supper?"

"Probably. There's . . . Well, I can't talk about it yet, Dan, because I promised Monty. You'll know soon enough."

"If there's trouble, you know I'll lend you a hand any-time."

"I know. Thanks." She grinned. "I kind of wish your uncle, Mr. Rodinbaugh, was here. He'd wade in and get to the bottom of this in two minutes."

"Hey, now, if you need a guy to back you up . . ."

"I've said too much, and I'm sorry. Don't worry, Dan, it's only a kind of minor mess. I want to find out more about it, or I won't sleep tonight. That's all."

"Okay," said Dan reluctantly, "but you know where to find me if you need me."

The threatening rain had begun as Julie pulled out of Deepwater Farm's long blacktop driveway and onto the main road: a sullen, slow, dark rain that matched the girl's mood. She was aware that she tended to dramatize some-times, that mysteries always seemed blacker in her imagina-tion than they were. But she knew that when she seriously felt trouble, when she smelled it in the wind and sensed it in the roughening of her skin into gooseflesh, then she'd better do something; and this morning she felt trouble even sharper than she had the day before at Greyhill Stud.

She discounted the worry over Bonnie. Of course, that was silly, a throwback to her early adventures with the great filly. But she was so disturbed about her new friend Pop Larrikin that she couldn't put her mind to anything else. He seemed—no, he *was*—such a fine person! And what-ever he had to do with the early-foaling deception, she wanted to know about it. About how and why he'd ever gotten snared into working at a place that would do such things.

The fact of the matter was that Julie Jefferson had a strong hunch that Pop Larrikin needed rescuing.

She snorted at herself. If she'd ever met a self-sufficient, capable man, it was Pop. And yet . . . Well, several times there'd been those odd pauses and remarks, as if he felt less than right about Greyhill. About Robert Lenkes and Nicholas Grey. Those hadn't been her imagination.

Half an hour on the way to the stud farm, she passed Mr. T's own horse-breeding domain, Fieldstone Farm. It was here that Bonnie had been born, in the days when old Monroe Bradley had had it. On an impulse, Julie turned in at the gate to visit with the foreman, Leon Pitt.

What Leon didn't know about the breeding and racing of thoroughbreds was hardly worth knowing. Perhaps he could help.

She found him in the main barn. "Julie, you're halfway to being drowned," he greeted her. "Dry off with this towel. How's your little beagle?"

"Thanks, Leon. She's fine; she's out in the car with her leather bone. We're on our way to Greyhill."

"Visiting Bonnie, are you?"

"Not today. I'm . . . I'm either playing detective, or butting in, and I'm not sure which."

"Tell me," he said simply, sitting down on a bale of straw.

She did, from the day when she'd delivered Bonnie to Lenkes. When she came to Pop, Leon interrupted.

"That would be the short little fella made of leather, little younger than me, eyes like warm emeralds and a nose that's hardly a nose at all, just a button. Talks four hundred words to the minute."

"That's Pop."

"I used to know him when he was at the track. Fact is, we were in the same training company during the war. I've always meant to go see him, but somehow never get around to it. A man drifts into habits like that and by-'n'-by he loses track of old buddies and never does find them again. How is Pop?"

"Oh, wonderful, but I think he's in trouble."

"Tell me," said Leon again, and listened carefully as she recapped her conversation with Pop, then Monty's discovery of the early foals. He was silent for a minute, chewing it over in his mind. "That isn't the Pop Larrikin I knew, putting up with something that isn't a hundred percent straight and narrow. But he could have his reasons. Or he might not know about it."

"How could that be possible?"

"Not everyone on a stud farm goes everywhere; you know that. A man has his job, and often his own territory, and if he's professionally restricted in the space he uses, he may never bother to walk over to the next barn, even, or the paddock beyond the hill. Now, Pop is Bothwell's handler, and believe me, he's a busy man enough with his duties. Could just be that he's never been in that particular barn. If he says he hasn't, when you ask him, then you can put money on it that he never has. You're a bright girl yourself, Julie, and full of inquisitive notions, and I s'pose you've seen every square foot of Deepwater. But hardly any grown man is that curious about things. It's a shame, but it's true. So what I'm saying is, if Pop gives you an answer that you can't believe—you go ahead and believe it! Even if it's that he knows nothing about any early foals."

"I don't understand how that could be possible. You'd know, Leon, if there was any sort of crime going on at Fieldstone."

"Well, sure I would, but I'm foreman! The whole place is my job. Pop, he's a stud groom. He may know, he may not. Depends on how much he's around that area, and whether Bothwell is the sire of some o' those foals. Naturally, if he is, then Pop would know; but it isn't a crime, Julie, it's—"

"That's what Monty said, but I don't understand. It's wrong isn't it?"

"Sure it's wrong. It's puttin' things over on people. But it's not like stealing, exactly."

"I don't care, I don't like it, and I can't believe that Pop Larrikin would do it! I think he's the kind of man who finds a dime in a telephone and puts it back in the slot instead of in his pocket. And if I'm wrong about him, I'll . . . I'll have to revise my opinions of the entire human race!"

Leon said patiently, "Let me try to explain this to you. If a man sets up to make books, like I always see you reading, about horses; and he prints 'em on cheap paper but he sell 'ems for a lot of money; well, then, he's maybe not being as honest as the fellow who prints his on good paper and sells for the same amount, but on the other hand, Julie, he isn't a crook. He's . . . well, he's cuttin' corners on you. So he's not doing you any favors, but he isn't precisely cheating you, either.

"Now, these Greyhill people, they're not cheating by much more than that amount of difference between cheap paper and good paper. And if an honest man had a job with them, and found out about the early foals, he might not like it, but he wouldn't feel he had to go runnin' to the police either. The police wouldn't be interested, any more'n they would in cheap paper in high-priced books. See?"

"Sort of. But a genuine three-year-old running as a two-year-old is going to have an edge over the others in the race. Even if the owner doesn't *know* that his colt's technically a three-year-old masquerading as a two. So it messes up racing. You can't argue me out of that."

"No, I can't. Eight months' difference in two horses, at least during their racing years, makes a real difference in strength and ability, and there's no denying it. And from the birthdays that Monty figured out for those foals, eight months' difference could be possible. But mostly there'd be maybe four or five." Leon shook his head. "Here I am trying to dope out an excuse for Pop Larrikin when I don't even know he needs one. Julie, you go ask him. But stay out of trouble, you hear me? And if you're still worried after you see Pop, come back here and talk."

"Thanks, Leon. I promise." She stood up and wrapped her raincoat around herself and belted it tightly.

"Oh, you might be on the lookout for a good stud groom," said Leon, almost too casually.

"Why?"

"Ol' Ackie Burke, he's got so stove up with arthritis that he has to move to Florida. So I'm minus a good man."

"Pop Larrikin is a good man."

"I don't need a small blond girl with a mere assistant trainer's status to inform me of what I've known for thirty years," said Leon loftily. "Gracious! Be tellin' me next how to read a horse's pedigree!"

Julie embraced him. "You *dear* Leon Pitt," she said, and raced out into the downpour.

By the time she reached the main gate of Greyhill Stud, the rain had stopped, though the morning was still roofed over with ash-colored clouds and had a sad, old feel to it. Inspector Vickel, with a black slicker thrown over his shoulders, came out and peered sharply at her.

"Are you here again?" he demanded, just as he had yesterday, though more irritated than ever. Lenkes must have chewed him out thoroughly, thought Julie. "What is it *this* time?"

"I want to come in and see—"

"No! No visitors during the breeding season! No gate passes except signed personal by Mr. Nicholas Grey himself!"

"But it isn't my horse, it's—"

"No! I ain't allowed to let nobody in without they got a gate pass!"

"Not nobody, not nohow?" inquired Julie innocently.

"Right! You can phone and ask about your mare if you have to, but I can't see what you think is gonna go wrong with her on a place like this," said the inspector, thrusting his rather beefy red face into the car at her. "Better still, we'll call you up when she's ready to come home. Visitors are not welcome!" he shouted, as she opened her mouth to object. "Especially visitors who come here busting up routine and cluttering up the place every single day!"

"Well, how about if you got in and rode with me to—"

He was taken aback, and showed it. "Ride? I don't ride with no one, kid. I don't even drive myself. Besides, I can't leave the gate. I got to keep out pests like you're being."

"Why don't you ride with anyone?"

"Because I get carsick is why. And airsick and seasick and *horse*sick, if you want to know." He backed off, looking as though he suspected her motives in asking him into a car, as though she wanted him to be deathly ill. "Now, you go home like a nice girl and don't come back again."

Julie rolled up her eyes, shrugged, and backed out. If he wouldn't even let her say that she wanted only to talk to Bothwell's handler, then she'd have to find another way in.

She had not come all this way only to be sent home as a nuisance.

She knew that Pop's house was on to the east, perhaps half a mile at most. There had been a simple dirt road running north-to-south beside his fenced pasture. That would probably be an access road leading to the main highway. It ought to be easy enough to find it.

"Though goodness knows, little beagle," she said aloud, "it wouldn's surprise me to find a ten-foot gate with five padlocks on it. I never saw such an armored, protected, defensive place in my life. Why, I'll bet they have a *moat* around their office!"

Greyhill, as she knew, covered some eighty-five hundred acres. Much of it, she discovered now, was naturally fenced by swamp, drainage ditches, woodland, thickets, and crop fields, with the usual white board fences barricading the land between. She drove for quite a distance until she realized that if there was an access road to Pop's place, she had missed it; she turned the car and went back more slowly, flicking her windshield wipers on and off occasionally as drops of rain plopped down from the trees and streaked her vision. Then she saw it, half-hidden at the edge of a sprawling thicket of low brush: a rough-surfaced dirt road, the worst holes in which had been partly filled with road metal—cinders, broken stone, and the like.

"Hang on, Nana dear," she said between solidly clenched teeth, and turned onto it cautiously. It lay perhaps two hundred yards up the highway from Greyhill's gate. It had to be the path to the small frame house where Pop lived.

The thing meandered. It must have originally been laid out, Julie thought, by a browsing cow. It dipped into hollows and turned around on itself until she was ready to shout "Straighten up!" at it. And then it rose over a hill, giving her a glimpse of the white house, and shot down into a basin among the hillocks, which, Julie saw barely in time, was full of muddy water. She squished to a halt on its verge. She crawled out of her car and stared at it, and dabbled in its murky depths with a stick.

It was ooze, and felt deep. The car had managed the troughs, potholes, ridges, and furrows of the road well enough, but this was beyond its powers.

"I go on alone from here, beagle-baby," she told Nana, who was jumping up and down on the seat and yipping. "You stay here and guard my car." She rolled the window down a couple of inches and locked the door and sloshed forward around the edge of the gigantic puddle.

The next easy rise showed her Pop Larrikin's place, and the first view of it stopped her in her tracks.

The crippled stallion, Scotch Tweed, stood in the paddock watching two men, who were just leaving with a led horse. One of the men was Pop, the other was a larger but much younger man, hardly more than a boy, who walked beside the horse, keeping an eye on its left foreleg. The horse moved at a sedate pace, throwing up its head now and again as it went.

Julie looked down at the scene, and felt bewilderment rush through her, accompanied by a kind of growing fear—fear of *what*, she didn't know. . . .

The second horse was Bonnie.

Chapter XI

It was noon when she got back to Fieldstone Farm, and twelve minutes after that before she found Leon at his cottage, eating lunch with his wife Mary Anne. She waved aside invitations to sit and have a bite, her words tumbling out helter-skelter until Mary Anne took her gently by the shoulders and pushed her down.

"You have a cup of tea, Julie, and a slab of cake, to keep up your strength while you tell him from the beginning," she ordered.

"Couldn't eat a thing . . . Pop had Bonnie at his place . . . and Inspector Vickel wouldn't let me in. . . ."

"Eat," said Leon.

"Not hungry," said Julie, picking up a fork. "There's big trouble, and I don't even know what it *is*." Just to be doing something with her hands, she cut off a piece of the thickly iced cake and put it in her mouth. Her taste buds were more aware of it than she was; before she'd noticed it, she'd eaten the entire slice, talking all the time. At last Leon began to make sense of the story.

"Sounds as if he's gone and mated her to his stallion. Otherwise, honey, I don't know what she'd have been doing there, no sir, I can't imagine what else." He scowled. "Maybe Pop's sort of gone funny in the head, all chafed and tormented in the mind as he's been over that ruined little horse of his. From what you told me about him, goin' on and on about how great Tweed could have been, how he wanted the blood passed down to posterity, I can't say I'm too surprised. That kind of thing weighs on a man fierce, 'specially when he lives alone." His hand found his wife's and held it tightly. "That's no way to exist. A man needs a good woman's advice and love to keep him on an even keel."

"He didn't seem at all crazy," objected Julie.

"Not crazy, just . . . I think 'eccentric' is the word I

101

want. He's been eight years with that horse, and six of them full of worry and disappointment."

"But what'll I *do?*" Julie asked plaintively.

Leon thought. "Monty's busy right now, and Mr. Tolkov is away somewhere, and that puts you in charge; she's your filly. You want my advice, I think it wouldn't hurt to go up there to Greyhill with a van and bring Bonnie back home, either here or to Deepwater. I just plain don't like anything about what I've heard!" he said, getting to his feet and pacing around the room. "I don't like the early foals, I don't like the nastiness of the guard and Lenkes, and I surely don't like Bonnie being taken over to Scotch Tweed!"

"Maybe he only wanted to introduce them to each other," Julie suggested rather helplessly.

"That's something a little kid would do, and you know it. This is serious, grown-up, racehorse business. Did you happen to notice if there were breeding hobbles in sight?"

"I wouldn't have noticed. I was struck stupid at the whole thing."

"Pop is Bothwell's handler. Suppose he said to himself, I'm gonna have my good old Tweed service Sunbonnet, instead of Bothwell, and when she's had a grand foal, I'll let everyone know my faith was justified—that would explain everything."

"But Pop is such a good, sane, kindly man," objected Julie.

"Still, he's a little cranky about his wonderful horse. And if there's another explanation, I can't imagine it," said Leon resolutely.

"Monty will be furious if I bring Bonnie home without his okay," she said. "He told me—"

"Monty Everett didn't know what sort of developments you were going to see this morning, Julie. Look here," said Leon, "it's only practical. Say Pop Larrikin intends to breed Bonnie to Scotch Tweed instead of Bothwell, and suppose it hasn't been done yet. Maybe she isn't far enough into her season yet. Maybe she won't settle to the first cover, or refused Tweed—lots of possibilities. Then it's *now* that you want to get her out of there!" He smacked a fist into one callused palm, hard. "Too much goin' on at Greyhill that isn't regular, Julie! You go bring her home."

"Leon Pitt, are you sending this child all alone into that

den of thieves?" demanded Mary Anne suddenly. "What kind of heartless act is that? You go along."

"I can't. I'm so short handed today that I shouldn't even have stopped for lunch. Darlin, she won't be in any danger," said Leon gently. "She can take up the old Bradley van and say she's bringing her filly home, and they'll just figure they saved eighteen thousand dollars and let her go. Pop Larrikin may have gone a shade overboard about that stallion of his, but he's no more dangerous than I am."

"Can you drive that antique horse van, Julie?"

"Sure, Mary Anne, I drove it from here to Deepwater last summer."

"It's in shape, and I'll see it's gassed up for you. That's my advice, Julie, and I'll back you against Monty or Tolkov or anyone," said Leon.

"And it's what I want to do," said the girl. "I won't sleep till Bonnie's back in her own stall."

"Neither will I," said Leon, but he said it to himself, not caring to frighten Julie any further.

As a matter of fact, Julie was not frightened in the least. She was terribly disappointed in her friend Pop, and she was angry as a wet bumblebee. But she was no more frightened than that same sopping insect.

Leon took her through the lowering, ashy day to where the van sat under a carport. It was a relic of the time when Monroe Bradley had owned Fieldstone Farm, and his retired colors, red and white, still decorated it, though the paint was chipped and peeling. It was a three-horse van with a double door on the left side, held by a barlock, which was a heavy metal bar that fitted into big lugs on either side. The van had the usual small windows on the sides, and a speaker system that allowed communication between the cab and the back.

Julie went to get Nana from her car while Leon filled the van's tank with gasoline. Nana was on a leash today, which she deeply and vocally resented.

"Remember how to use those five gears?"

"Leon, I could do it in my sleep," said Julie with vast confidence, and climbed in, waved good-bye, started the rig up, rolled smoothly away, declutched, put it in neutral, let out the clutch, reengaged—at least, that was what she had meant to do; but forgetting to double-clutch, she succeeded in producing a loud and horrible noise of grinding gears.

Feeling herself blush, she glanced in he rear-view mirror at Leon, who was bending over with helpless laughter.

"I guess the thinks I *did* do it in my sleep," she said. humbly to the beagle. "At least I amused him, and he can stand some amusing about now!"

She took the van over the wet highway at the same brisk clip at which she drove her own car, and was back at Greyhill's gates a little after two in the afternoon, only to run into a mile-high stone wall in the person of red-faced Inspector Vickel.

"No!"

"But—"

"No! You got no prior permission from Mr. Grey, you go no right to bring that trailer in here and—"

"It's not a trailer, it's a van."

"I don't care if it's a covered wagon!" roared the much-enduring guard. "You gotta have a gate pass, especially for a horse!"

"That's silly. You know perfectly well that it's my own horse."

"But there isn't any prior arrangements! Why," he said, lowering his voice and trying to look like a reasonable man who was totally in the right, "why, little girl, do you have to make my job so tough? What did I ever do to you? Go home. Telephone to Mr. Nicholas Grey. Tell *him* what you want to do. He'll issue you a pass. I'll have it here in the—"

"Call him now and get one, then," said Julie. "I'm not going to trundle this van all the way to Deepwater and back to save you a simple phone call."

"Mr. Grey himself just went out that gate not ten minutes ago, and won't be back for hours!" Inspector Vickel paused and, obviously, thought hard. "Maybe days," he said hopefully. "I don't know where he's gone. So turn around and leave. Please."

"Get Robert Lenkes, then. He can pass Bonnie for me. He'll be happy to see the last of us," said Julie. "He'll thank you for getting him."

"No he won't, neither. He's out away from the barns someplace. No telephone within miles. Go home."

"Not without my filly."

"You can't have your filly without they tell me you can." He raised his hands to the leaden skies and asked in a kind of shriek, "How did I ever get mixed up with you, anyway?

Why can't you behave like the other owners? They bring in their mares, and they leave 'em quietly and go home. They don't show up every day to hold their mares' hooves. They don't bring trailers or vans or railroad trains to take their mares home right at the start of breeding season. They don't turn a perfectly good stud farm into a nursery school. They leave me *alone!*"

Julie stared at him silently until he began to fidget. At last she said, "Why don't you want me to come in and get my filly? Is something wrong with her? Are you hiding some secret here at Greyhill?"

He pushed his beefy face up as far as he could, which, as he was a short man and it was a tall cab, was somewhat less effective than he intended. "Just what do you mean by that?"

"You are acting very suspiciously. I believe I will go down the road and put in a call to my employer, Mr. Tolkov, who owns Deepwater Farm and is a pillar of the turf."

"*I* know who Mr. Tolkov is! *He* wouldn't show up here every day to see his dingaling filly!" The guard looked around carefully, as though agents of the mighty Tolkov could just be lurking nearby. "I bet he doesn't know that some little girl is always showing up to annoy me to death," he muttered. His voice was less assured than it had been.

"Well, if you'll simply let me go and get Sunbonnet—"

"Look, I can't do that. I honest and true can't. It ain't legal."

"Certainly it's legal. If you keep her here instead of giving her to me, *that* isn't legal."

"Well, the rules are, I can't give out any horse without orders; and if doing that is legal, I don't understand the meaning of the word," he said stubbornly.

Julie, after seeing that Nana's leash was snugly wound about the opposite door handle, opened her side and got down from the cab. "Well, can you do me a favor, then?" she asked. "Can you check on my speaker system?"

"What speaker system?" he said dubiously.

"The intercom between the cab and the back. I don't know whether it works, and it has to." She took the bar of the double door and swung it up free of the legs, opened one side, and gazed at the guard piteously. "It just *has* to," she said.

"Why?"

"So I can talk to my horse when I get her, naturally."

"But you ain't getting her."

"I am eventually. Do you think Mr. Grey is going to keep her? Are you saying he's some kind of criminal?"

"No!" Inspector Vickel peered suspiciously into the dim depths of the van. "Where is it?"

"Up front there. Just get in and speak to me."

"I don't even like these things when they're standing still," he grumbled, but he hoisted himself up in and took a couple of steps forward. When the door closed tightly behind him, she could hear him emit a startled squawk of protest. She dropped the bar into place and got into the cab again.

"Inspector Vickel?"

"What's the idea?" said her grilled speaker in a raspy bleat. "What's going on here?"

"I am going to get my horse, Sunbonnet. Are you comfortable?"

"NO!" roared the speaker.

"Now, Inspector Vickel—"

"Whadda you keep saying that for?" demanded the voice, its owner torn between dismay at being in the van and irritable wonder at the phrase. "I *got* no vickel. It's *your* vickel."

"Well, I don't know your name," said Julie with flawless logic. "I am going to the barren-mare barn. I know you get carsick, so I'll go very slowly. Hold on to one of the pillars at the front of the partitions and you'll hardly feel a thing. It's only about a quarter of a mile."

"No!" said the voice, a kind of growing horror in its tone. "That's kidnapping!"

"It most certainly isn't. I only want you to accompany me to the barn so that you can tell Mr. Grey I didn't steal a halter or damage anything, but only took my filly. If you weren't so stubborn," said Julie severely, "I wouldn't have to do this. But there's something about this farm that's wicked and improper, and I don't intend to leave Bonnie here a minute longer than necessary. Are you holding on tight?"

"You can't do this to me!" blatted the speaker. "My heart—"

"I can too." Carefully she put the van in gear and rolled down the road at some three miles an hour. "Okay so far?"

"Let me out of this vickel!"

"Vehicle," said Julie, but under her breath so as not to embarrass the poor man. "Hang on, here's a dip."

"Oh, no, no, no," said the imprisoned guard in a feebler voice than before. "Little girl, you don't know how this makes me feel."

"I am very sorry. I apologize. Will you let me go quietly up to the barn and retrieve Sunbonnet if I let you out here?"

"You got no pass. It's illegal. And you're kidnapping me."

"Not when you're only on your own territory. I'm just saving my filly from being horsenapped."

"That is the dumbest thing I ever heard of in twenty years of working with a long line of noodle-headed horse owners," said the intercom vehemently, and then gulped. "Lemme out," it said.

"If you promise not to interfere with my constitutional rights."

"What?"

"If you let me take my horse."

"I can't. No! I know my rights!"

"And I know mine," said Julie, and went up a rise and down a long slow descent, the barns in sight. "Almost there," she said brightly.

"Oof," said Inspector Vickel. "I'm a sick man."

Julie remembered the night when Mr. T had taken his first and only ride in the back of a horse van. He had mentioned several times thereafter that he would not repeat the episode for a thousand dollars, tax-free. Inspector Vickel seemed to have the same opinion of the experience. It *was* rather like riding in a roller coaster that had lost one wheel, though Julie herself, who loved roller coasters, had never minded it.

"This is mean," she said to herself as the intercom made desperate, unintelligible noises, "but I have to take Bonnie, and that man simply won't listen to reason."

She drew up beside the barn where the filly had been staying. A stableman came out and walked toward her quickly. He was a stranger to her, and a very rough-looking type. Automatically she pushed down the door lock and rolled her window up half a foot. "I'm here to get Sunbonnet," she called to him.

"Let's see your pass."

"I don't have one. Mr. Grey is out, and Mr. Lenkes can't be found."

"I don't know you," said the man. He stepped onto the running board of the cab. She rolled up the window a little farther.

"I'm Julie Jefferson. I own Sunbonnet."

"Yeah? I can't hand out a valuable mare without a pass, kid." He scowled as the intercom burst into passionate but incomprehensible speech. "Turn your radio down."

"I don't have a radio. Please bring Sunbonnet out here. Carefully," said Julie, afraid and angry at the same time.

"Can't do it, kid. Say, how come you got past the gate without a pass?"

"Because she kidnapped me is why!" bellowed the intercom.

"What was that?"

"I'm in this here vickell!"

"Who's that?" said the man, peering into the cab past Julie. "You got a talking beagle there?"

"No, she's got *me!*" howled the speaker in its weird, artificial human tones. "Gemme outa here! I could *die* in here!"

"What's going on, kid? Suppose you get out and explain this whole thing," said the stableman curtly.

"I want my filly."

"Well, tell it to Lenkes. He'll be back in half an hour or so."

"I want her *now.*"

"You can't have a horse without a pass! You some kind of kook?" Then he raised an arm as though to reach in and unlock the door, and Julie panicked. She ground the gears and got the van moving again, and the man, probably startled by the awful racket, jumped off and back. Julie wheeled onto a farm-machine road that led toward Pop Larrikin's house, or at least in that general direction. She was scared; she needed someone who, no matter how obscure his motives and actions were, was a friend and would listen to her. She needed Pop at her side.

The stableman was yelling something at her, and the guard in the back of the van was yowling and gurgling alternately, sounding both furious and terrified. Julie, as rattled as she ever had been, drove off over the rough road and down a steep short grade, and the barns disappeared behind her.

"HELP!" said the prisoner at full volume.

"I'm sorry, very sorry," said Julie, "but I can't stop yet. That man was not looking nice at all."

"Aarrgh!" replied Vickel. "Listen, stop. Stop! My heart—"

"It's your stomach, I imagine," said Julie.

"No, I got a condition!"

The truck listed to one side as she said this, slammed over a badly rutted place, gave a leap, and bounced heavily down into a trough of muck. Julie, clinging to the wheel and breathing heavily, concentrated on keeping them upright; she had not really understood what he'd just said. "If you people were honest," she exclaimed, "this wouldn't have happened. I never intended to give you a bad time. I only wanted my filly."

"How'd you get to know about it, I'l like to know," said a voice-from-the-tomb whimper from the speaker.

Julie, despite her troubles with the bouncing van and her fear of the strange, belligerent personnel of Greyhill Stud, began to think at a brisk clip. At last she said, "Never mind. What I want is a confession from you."

A deep, whiny gulp resounded in her ear. "You know you'll be up on a murder charge if I die back here?"

"It isn't as bad as it feels, really."

"But my heart is gonna bust wide open!"

"No, no, you'll be fine. I just want the facts about the early foals and—"

"Oh, help," he groaned, thrashing around so wildly that she thought he would tear out the partitions. "I can't stand this. Lemme out. Please."

"After a few simple words. I'm waiting." She double-clutched into the lowest gear. "Tell me what's going on at Greyhill."

They struck a tree branch and skidded sideways and jolted back onto the road with a jerk that was upsetting even to Julie, who was practically immune to motion sickness.

"Crazy . . . the kid's plain crazy . . . out to kill me . . . okay! You hear me, girl? I'll tell you! Get me outa this in one piece before my heart explodes on me! Whaya wanna know?"

"Everything," said Julie, remorseless.

"Early foals," he said in a gasp that sounded all but final. "They try for late November. Always have, long's I been here. The studs—oh!—you want to hear about them?"

"Yes," said Julie, and added on a sudden impulse, "Bothwell."

"Great horse on the track," said the voice, definitely green in tone. "Ah! Oh! My heart, it's dying on me!"

"Don't be silly. Bothwell."

"Stands for biggest fee on the place, but his produce record's phony."

Julie blinked and slowed down. She had no wish to make the poor man genuinely sick. They were hidden from everyone here, surrounded by hills. "Phony," she repeated, amazement kept out of her voice with an effort.

"Fake. Most of his get isn't his. Ouch!" There was a crash and a groan. Startled, she brought the van almost to a halt, but then the captive Vickel spoke again. "Even Hepburn's Earl," he said, naming a flashy colt, supposedly by Bothwell out of Scotland Mary, who was setting some records of his own at the Florida tracks, "he's by one o' the other studs."

"One of the others?" She could think of nothing to say, except for repetitions of these incredible confessions.

"Yeah. Dunno which. Bothwell, they book more mares to him than he can handle, you know, reasonable-like, every year. You realize that I'm gonna die? Help me!"

"Right away," said Julie, coasting gently along an upward slope. "Why do they do that?"

"He hasn't produced such almighty wonderful foals these past few years." Abruptly it all came in a great rush, as from a man who truly felt himself to be slipping away from life and wanted to unburden his conscience. "They got to keep his fee up, after all. He's the big money-earner in this place. So more'n likely most of his get is some other nag's. They keep his book full, but breed most of the mares to younger stallions. Good enough studs, too, but not in his class." There was a pale chuckle. "Bothwell himself isn't in his own class, if people only knew. It's all a big cover-up. Cash keeps rolling in. Only now it'll stop. Ghah! Who cares?"

"Is the whole staff in on both . . . both swindles?" she asked. "Like Pop Larrikin and Lenkes and all?"

"Larrikin is Bothwell's handler; what do you think? Lenkes and Grey are the guys . . . run everything. Some grooms . . . and the trainer, they get bonuses. Rest of us just do our jobs and shut up."

Julie, wholly absorbed in the revelation and her tangled feelings, stepped on what she thought was the brake; it was the gas. The van tore up the last few yards of the slope, shot over the crest, and sailed down the other side between the hay fields on either hand. Then the road lifted itself under her like a long snake rising gradually from the earth, until it was merely the crown of a ridge, with the fields a yard or two beneath it; and although Julie was going no more than eight miles an hour, the wet surface and the twists in the hogback made it difficult to hold the old van on the road. Vainly she tried to slow down, the mistreated gears shrieking.

"Murder!" screamed the imprisoned guard pitifully.

The horse van hit a muddier place than it had touched before. It slewed to the right, even as it was slowing down, and the wheels on that side suddenly dropped off the naturally crowned road. The van went over the edge with a horrible crash and hung there precariously, teetering slowly back and forth, deciding whether to settle with its undercarriage firmly on the road or to tip all the way over sidelong and fall the ten feet straight down into the hay field below.

There was a moment of silence as the right wheels spun to a stop and the red-and-white van tilted gently from side to side. Nana yipped anxiously. Julie closed her eyes and felt frozen. Then from the intercom there came a shattering scream of pure animal terror.

Chapter XII

The Greyhill guard, thrown heavily against the leather-covered foam rubber that cushioned the sides of the stall in which he had been trying to maintain a most uncertain balance, had grabbed a chain and a pillar made of pipe, thus saving himself from sprawling headlong for what would have been the third time. Clutching the metal tightly, he had looked up and out of the left window. All that he could see was the flat lead color of the afternoon sky. A glance down at the opposite window had shown him a field of hay, evidently far beneath him. A horrible pain had constricted his chest, and he had emitted the shriek of a lifetime.

Carefully Julie unhooked Nana's leash from the right door handle and tucked the fat little dog under her arm. Cautiously she opened her door and slid onto the running board. The van jerked slightly, but held. She stepped to the slippery road and hurried back to unbar the double doors and pull them open, Nana left safely anchored with her leash under a rock.

In the haggard creature who gazed out at her, she had some difficulty in recognizing her old acquaintance Inspector Vickel. His complexion was the color of a piece of well-watered lawn. His mouth seemed permanently open, and his eyes were glazed and wet. His pudgy hands shook visibly as he gripped the pillar and the chain.

"Heart," he said.

"What?"

"Heart. Terrible. I got a bad heart."

"Come over here carefully and I'll help you down," said Julie. She realized now what the poor soul had been trying to impress on her during all these minutes—had it been only minutes? yes, no more than three or four—while she had blithely been tossing him around like a ball in the horse

113

van. He had a heart condition. "Come on," she said urgently.
"Walk over slowly."

"Can't move," he croaked. "Dying."

"No, you're not. You're scared," she said, praying that it
was true. "Just take a few steps. Please hurry!"

He writhed. "I can't move," he said plaintively. "I don't
dare."

Julie sucked in a deep breath and hoisted herself into the
van. It rocked back and forth twice before it settled. Ever
so gently she moved to his side. His fingers were clamped
on the metal, immovable.

"Pocket," he said, "shirt pocket. Pills. Heart."

"Oh dear," she said, and unbuttoned his uniform jacket
and fished out a small tin of medicine. She saw the label.
"These are stomach pills," she said blankly, "for heartburn."

"Yeah, but they help my heart. Put two in my mouth."

Obediently she stuck a couple of tablets onto his tongue.
"I've seen nitroglycerin pills, and these aren't—"

"Need a prescription for them," he said, chewing slowly.
"I'd have to see a doctor."

"You mean you have a bad heart and you don't ever see
a doctor?"

He was standing there sweating and shuddering, his eyes
closed. "That's right."

"Why?"

"Oh," he said, his voice a husky mumble, half-ashamed,
"I guess I'm scared to."

"But how do you know your heart's bad?"

"Hurts."

"Where?"

"Here," he said, and let go of the chain and thumped his
chest and then renewed his terrified grip.

"But that's your stomach, I think," said Julie, not your
heart!"

"What do you know?" he said, gritting his teeth audibly.

"More than you, I'm afraid. You get pains when you eat
too much, or when you're worried, don't you?" The man
nodded. "Don't you know you could be developing an ulcer?"
She caught his shoulder briefly as the van tilted again. "Come
on, I'll help you out."

"If we move, this thing's going over," he said faintly.

"If we don't move, it will. Come on. One foot, then the

other." She managed to pry his fingers off the pillar. "Hold my hand."

He opened his eyes, stared at her, and evidently found his courage somewhere below all the fright and resignation. She led him toward the door. "You get out first," she said.

"No, you. You're only a kid, for gosh sake."

"You're a sick man," she said almost harshly. "I don't know if you have a bad heart or only an upset stomach, but you're sick, and I did it to you. Now jump out!"

Inspector Vickel gripped the side of the door with one shaking, pudgy hand. He collected himself and leaped into space, going with a spludge to hands and knees in the thin mud of the road. "Come on!" he shouted.

Julie jumped down beside him. The van tipped a trifle farther, then righted itself and settled.

He gazed up at her, trembling. She had never seen anyone look so ill. She felt miserable that she had inflicted this on him, even though she had not meant to do so. She had an intense desire to run away before he could summon his strength and commence beating her up. But she knew that whatever he might do to her, she had deserved it; and she could not abandon a sick man.

"I apologize, I do, honestly," she said to him. "But I don't believe you have a heart condition at all, if you've never had it checked by a doctor. It sounds to me exactly like an ulcer. Maybe it's only beginning. How long have you had pains?"

"Years," he said, struggling with her help to his feet. She led him over to a log, which was lying rather dangerously close to the wheel ruts along the left side of the road, and made him sit on it.

"You'll feel better in a minute," she said. "I want you to promise me that you'll see a doctor right away about those pains. I don't believe they're your heart at all, not if those stomach pills fix them. Tell me you will."

"You ever know anybody with a bad heart, kid?"

"Yes, I have. And with ulcers too. And I don't have any training in things like this, only where horses are concerned, but from everything I ever heard," said Julie briskly, patting his wet face with her own handkerchief, "I'd diagnose your trouble as plain old too-much-fat-and-nerves. So please say you'll go to a doctor."

He blinked. "Maybe I will, at that. I thought you got

stomach pains down here," he said, patting his bulging belly.

"That is nonsense," said Nurse Julie Jefferson firmly.

"Honest?"

"Honest."

"I been scared of doctors half my life."

"So are a lot of people. But you go to one and see. Anyway," she said, "I do want you to know I'm sorry, I'd never even have shut you up in that van if I'd known you had *any* sort of . . . of condition."

"I haven't felt this awful since I got decoyed into that rowboat," he said, "and that's twenty years ago. Zhzhzhzh! Well. I guess I'll make it okay." His face was slowly resuming its natural hue, beet-red. "I cut my own throat in there, didn't I? Spilled it all to you." He looked up at her again. "What's it matter?" he said philosophically. "You saved my life. I owe you."

"I'll never say that you told me," Julie assured him. "I promise, if *you'll* promise to go to a doctor."

"Okay, I will. You just gimme new hope, little girl." He sighed. "Nobody ever told me you could get stomach pains away up here. I thought that was your heart and maybe your liver, and my family's had heart problems forever."

"Maybe you do too, but *do* find out!"

He regarded her a little blankly. "Why would you care what happens to me?"

"Well, for heaven's sake, you're a human being, and you never hurt me! I gave you a bad time mostly by accident."

"Yeah. Well, I guess you did. How'd you catch on to what was going on at Greyhill, anyway?"

"Oh," said Julie, "I happened to see things I wasn't meant to see when I was here last."

"I tried to keep you out. They can't say I didn't try."

"You did your very best."

"And got rattled around like a pebble in a jar for my trouble. I'm gettin' too old for this crazy business," he said, shaking his head; he looked about forty. "I'm gonna get a nice quiet job in a auto body shop."

Julie was again thinking of what he had told her. "Why doesn't anyone tell the authorities what's going on here?" she asked him. "Why don't they tell the Jockey Club, or the other owners?"

"What good would that do? Nobody'd ever tell except if

he wanted, ah"—the man struggled to recollect the word—
"revengeance. There wouldn't be a reward to collect, you
know. Everybody here would lose their jobs, and nobody
wants that. 'Course, you get the drifters, the birds that pick
up a job as exercise boys for a couple months and then dis-
appear, or get fired for drinking. Maybe they might want to
make trouble for Grey or the rest. So if they tell, who'd believe them? Besides, the pay's good." The guard stood up
and tested his legs. He looked as well as ever. "Hey," he said,
glancing sideways at her, "you're some kinda detective, huh?"

"Very amateurish," said Julie absently. "Well, I'm sorry I
had to bring you all the way out here and strand you, but I
can't drive you back, obviously."

"That's okay, I can walk back. I walk a lot. Good for the
heart. Tell you what, I'll have the boys come and put this
vickel on its feet for you."

"I suppose it'll take a wrecker with a winch," said Julie,
eyeing the tipped van.

"Couple of tractors with hooks'll do it, one to pull forward
and one to the left." He stared straight at her for a moment.
It was clear that to him she was quite unbelievable. "You
really won't tell anybody it was me that filled you in on how
things operate here?"

"Of course not," said the girl miserably. She was thinking
now of Pop Larrikin. "I only want my filly."

"You can get a pass for her when Lenkes gets back. He
was complainin' about you yesterday to Grey, anyhow. Be
glad to see the last of you." He looked at her for a moment.
"Oh," he said, "we were on borrowed time for the last ten
years. The game was about played out. I got no call to be
sore at you." Surprisingly, he thrust out his hand. "No hard
feelings. You put it over on me very neat."

She shook his hand. "Good luck, Inspec—I mean, sir."

She watched him stride up the road, wobbling a little from
side to side. It occurred to her that some time would pass
before her van could be rescued from its perch above the
hay field. If she could find Pop's place, she would have a
few words with him. Perhaps he would tell her why he had
been a party to such downright immoral proceedings.

Leaving the keys in the van, she walked down the long
hogbacked road, Nana tugging furiously at her leash and
woofing at occasional sparrows. Julie was unsure about her
directions, and the sun was so hidden behind the thick

masses of black and dull-silver clouds that she could see no hint of it. She came to the next rise and trudged upward, and there on the left ahead was the small frame house. This was the road that led past Pop's place and on to the highway.

She opened the gate and walked up to the door and knocked, and there was no answer. She tried the handle, for despite all her suspicion, she still thought of Pop as a friend; but the door was locked. Aimlessly, she went around the house and out to the barn.

Two horses turned their heads to look at her. The nearest was Tweedy; the other must be Pop's new "aging mare"— what was her name? Kimberley Gem. Julie strolled over to say hello.

And Nana, excited as only a puppy can get, began to bark.

Kimberley Gem, though Julie did not know this until later, had been a resident of Pop's barn for no more than twenty-four hours. She had come a long way and she was still skittish, her nerves ready to jerk at the smallest thing: a blowing bit of paper, a bird flying through the stable, and especially a yapping puppy. Rolling her eyes up till the whites gleamed like thick frost in the shadows of the unlit stable, the mare flung up her heels and kicked out with her powerful legs, revolving in a wild circle in the confines of the stall. The clatter was terrifying, and the motion so fast that Julie could scarcely follow it. She snatched up Nana and clamped a firm, gentle hand over the dog's jaws. But the damage was done.

Whirling around, the mare sent her rear hooves slamming with great force against the half-door. It was accidental, certainly—the animal in its momentary alarm was not trying to break out, but only to express its consternation—but when the door, its flimsy hook ripped from the old wood, flew open with a crash, Gem had already whipped around to face it, and came charging out into the barn like a racer from the starting gate. Skidding, stumbling, and making a tremendous racket with her plates, she brushed by Julie and shot out into the open.

Julie muffled a wail of despair, gasped as she steadied herself, moved as quickly but smoothly as possible to the stall where Tweedy was cocking his marvelous head and showing the whites of *his* eyes, and said to him, "There, there, old boy, it's nothing, it's just a silly mare taking a run. You aren't afraid, are you? No, there's a good boy . . ." and a few other endearments. Tweedy quieted at once. He was not used to such shenanigans in his own barn, but he had seen horses lose their cool before today.

"Well, you're all right," said Julie thankfully. "Now, let's see if we can catch the Gem before she . . . Oh, wow!" It had struck her that the mare might run straight out onto the highway. "I've got to hurry," she told the beagle, dashing outside with it in her arms, its muzzle still held closed against more barks. "Oh, if you were only a little older and more reliable!"

The mare was galloping away toward the south, as Julie had feared. Not daring to call to her, Julie ran down the road behind her, heart in mouth and Nana gripped snugly in both arms. Gem followed the track for a time, until it began to rise, and then canted off left into a place of rock outcrops and folded little hills.

"If she loses herself or is hurt, I'll be to blame. Why did I ever haul you into that stable?" She tentatively released the pup's mouth, and was rewarded with the beginning of a loud, shrill, impudent bay of protest. The little beast found itself stifled again.

"First the van, and now this. Oh, what a day," said Julie, heading out across land that gave soggily beneath her feet. The mare had vanished. Julie came to the place where she'd seen her last, and there was no sign nor sound to indicate where she'd gone.

Julie set the beagle on its feet. "Redeem yourself," she told it sternly, "and fetch that horse!" She took her hand from the whimpering face, another bay started, and Nana recoiled with amazement as her mistress tapped her sharply on the nose with her fingertips. "Hush! No yelling. Find the horse." Nana gazed up with brown eyes full of sorrow. "It's your fault, you silly puppy! Now, grow up fast, and find Julie that mare." Nana looked around vacantly, and sniffed a penetrating sniff. "You aren't even trying," said Julie. "I'm just out of my head to trust you, but I have to." She unsnapped the leash. "Go fetch. Go on, find the nice mare. And don't bark at it when you do!"

At last Nana went off at her rolling sailor's run, Julie right behind her. She headed down to the southeast between two hillocks, and the wildest optimist would hardly have believed that she was following a trail of scent. However, when the two of them came out on the other side of the shallow valley, the truant mare was standing about fifty yards off, looking back at them over her shoulder.

"Heel, Nana," said Julie. Nana trotted briskly forward toward the horse.

"Oh, no," said Julie, brushing wisps of blond hair out of her eyes. "You roly-poly little sausage," she said fiercely, and broke into a run that she tried to make as friendly and un-menacing as she could. Gem went away, first at a walk, then, as Nana drew near, at a canter. She may have been aging, but she had a couple of pecks of energy left in her, thought the girl. What to do?

"I don't even have a halter with me," she reminded herself aloud, "and I don't know what sort of temperament this lady has. I should have listened to Monty. . . ."

The mare turned to the right and went down a slope that Julie from behind could not see yet, and then disappeared once more.

Nana, mercifully silent but with all her fat puppy instincts for trailing plain to see, her ears flopping and her head high, turned the same corner and was also lost to view.

Julie sprinted to the slope and turned and stopped dead. Before her, hidden from every point of vantage except the place where she stood, with thickets of brush and scrubby trees concealing it save for this one narrow place, was the mouth of a large and forbidding limestone cave.

And there was nowhere else for the mare and the dog to have gone.

There are many limestone caves in this part of Kentucky; indeed, there were some in the northwestern section of Julie's own Deepwater Farm, which Mr. T had told her were still unexplored. As far as Julie was concerned, they could remain that way forever; she had gone so far as to peek into them with a flashlight, while standing at the entrances, but she did not like the looks of them and saw no reason whatever to explore their depths. Julie Jefferson was a firm believer in sunlit meadows and places without walls.

The rich loam of the Bluegrass region is all underlaid with decomposing limestone, through which old rivers and even small streams have cut long series of caverns through the centuries. Some of them are deep, great eroded underground valleys that happen to be covered by stone roofs. Some are so shallow that a person can enter, if at all, on hands and knees only. Some are now dry, while others still contain the rivers and brooks that formed them. Some have enormous stalactites dripping from the rough ceilings; others hoard the bones of beasts and men who lived there in prehistoric times.

This one, as Julie saw when she had scrambled down the soggy approach to it, was about seven feet high at the opening, and slightly less wide. It was black as starless night within. Julie examined the marshy ground that ended a little short of the cave. Yes, both Nana and Gem had gone straight into it! How could they see in there?

She walked just inside and waited, but she heard nothing, and her vision did not adjust to any helpful degree. At last she called, "Nana! Come here, Nana!" Her voice writhed into the depths and came rolling back to her in too-loud echoes—*Na-na-na-na!* That would frighten the already scared mare. She daren't repeat it. Besides, there was no answering bark.

She thought hard for a few seconds, and then, realizing that she had to go in after the animals, that there was no alternative, she turned and ran like a long blue-jeaned rabbit, up the slope and back across the field, between the low hills, over the wet, soggy place and past the rock outcrops, to the road and northward like a miler at her best pace till she came to Pop's again. There was no sign that he had returned, so she headed without pause for the barn.

Tweedy gave her an inquiring look. "Good boy," she panted, searching the place hurriedly, "good little horse, oh, you fine little chestnut face." She threw a halter over her arm and then found what she had been almost certain she recalled seeing there: a battered old three-cell flashlight on a shelf. At the push of her finger it clicked and a strong white beam shot out. The batteries were fresh.

Whee-ew!

"Bye, Tweedy boy," she said, and went back toward the limestone cave at the same breakneck rate.

A runaway horse van and a runaway horse all in the same hour, to say nothing of a lost puppy, was very close to being too much. But Julie, having no time or inclination to sit down and cry, tore over marshy fields and past rocks and hills till she reached the cave entrance once more. There, without a pause, she snapped on the flash and dived into the forbidding hole.

She was surrounded by walls of pale, dull white, streaked

and splotched on most surfaces with gray, black, and even blue tints, which were caused by impurities in the limestone. The whole place looked to her as though someone had dug a passageway through an enormous cake, and then iced the walls of the passage with thick gooey frosting, which had then melted slightly and gotten rather dirty. She laid a hand tentatively on one wall; it was cold, though not intensely so, and slightly moist to her touch. The air was cool and fresh. Along one side of the lumpy, smooth floor ran the remains of what might have once been a strongly flowing stream of water, now only a three-inch-wide rivulet, clear and moving slowly into the depths.

Julie went a dozen feet and stopped and shone the torch straight ahead. The tunnel bent left and disappeared a little way beyond where she stood. She listened hard: nothing.

She went on, turned the bend, found to her relief that the grotto did not branch, but continued on its slightly downhill course as wide and as high as it had been at the entrance. Julie followed it, watching the floor for possible tripping places and the aisle ahead for signs of life. Her own light footsteps brought muffled echoes, like the footfalls of questing mice within the walls of an old house at midnight—an old house in some grotesque amusement park, she thought, looking at the wierd frozen-ooze surfaces all about her.

She was beginning to feel the crawl of fright along her arms and down her back. This was a terribly creepy place. She switched her mind off that topic instantly. There was a spooked horse and a simpleminded beagle to rescue. And if this channel separated into two or more passages, or widened into one of those vast halls full of stalactites, stalagmites, and pools and streams and pits and hidden places, well, then she would be in real trouble.

As though I'm not already, she said to herself, thinking briefly of Bonnie and the menacing personnel of Greyhill. . . . The job now was to go forward, not to chatter in her head about what might happen or what was going on far above her, but to move into the cavern and find the beasts.

How under the sun—or under the earth—had they found their way? She turned off the flashlight for an instant, and utter, thick, horrible blackness shut down all about her. Julie snapped it on again at once. She remembered a horse at St. Clair's who had had to be led forcibly into any stable that wasn't brilliantly lit. Gem was apparently at the other end of the horse scale, and liked pitch-dark places.

The walls were narowing.

Could that be her imagination? No, she realized that the roof was only a couple of inches above her head, and that she could touch the wall on either side without straightening her arms fully. Soon, if this kept on, there would be barely room for her to pass through, let alone a horse.

Could the animals have gone out into the daylight while she was over at Pop Larrikin's? She hadn't thought to check the footprints at the entrance the second time.

At least there was, so far, no danger of losing her way.

How far had she come? She ought to have counted her paces. But what good would that have done? Ten yards or a mile, she'd have had to negotiate this limestone burrow anyway.

Something touched her on the shoulder, and she gave a smothered yip of fear. The flash showed her a projecting lump of blue-gray stone. She drew a deep breath. At least the air was still good. But the gloom beyond her torch's reach was awful. And there were even more echoes now, whether all from her footfalls or from something else, she couldn't guess.

Funny, she'd have expected it to grow colder as the cave descended, but the temperature seemed exactly the same.

Funny, she'd also expected that she would be trembling with dread of the unknown by now, and . . . and, well, she *was*.

There was a sound ahead that stopped her in her tracks. It was metal on rock, that clink that is unlike any other sound. She held the flashlight up and shot it forward. At the extreme range of its beam, she saw something moving.

Dropping the shaft of light toward the passage in front of her feet, she hurried forward as fast as she could manage to travel. It had to be Kimberley Gem. It had looked large and brown. She must not startle the mare by shining the bright torch directly at her.

The silly fear was gone. Now Julie was aware only of caution, hope, and the knowledge that the tunnel was only about three and a half feet wide. If Gem had stopped, it must be because she had been jammed, or was about to be jammed if she took another few steps. And Julie, whose basic good sense had triumphed over panic without her even being aware

of it, went down the eerie aisle with her head full of plans on
how to get the mare out of here—none of which seemed
possible.

She was almost to the place where Gem stood. She shone
the torch at her own feet, the reflections from the walls and
roof showing her a large and sweaty horse just ahead. They
also showed her that the ceiling was higher here; apparently,
during some ancient time, a long section of limestone had
caved in and fallen to the depths of the river below, which
had gradually washed it along its then-full channel and dis-
integrated it, for the floor was as smooth here as behind her.

Gem was not caught by the walls, but if she moved on
much farther, she would be. She must have moved through
the cavern this long by the touch of one wall or the other,
probably quite slowly. It was an odd thing for a horse to do.
But then, horses often do things that seem incredibly odd,
acts that may appear right to the horse and utterly mad to
humans. That is because, as Leon sometimes reminded Julie,
no person, be she ever so horse-minded, can truly think like
a horse.

Julie spoke to Gem in a soft, soothing tone. The mare, who
had pricked up her ears at the sound of Julie's movements,
now turned her head and looked backward with one suspicious eye. There was no room on either side for Julie to
pass her and get to the other end of her. A gentle pull on the
tail would earn Julie a perfectly deserved set of hooves in the
stomach. There was no vocal way to impress on Gem that
she must back up.

Julie set the flashlight carefully on the level portion of
the floor, its beam aimed upward. This created a fairly soft
all-over glow in the stone hallway, so that Julie could see
everything for some yards ahead and behind. Only then did
she glimpse Nana, a small beagle sitting just in front of Kimberley Gems' forelegs. The puppy was as still and silent as
the limestone, her gaze steady on the mare's head.

"For goodness' sake," breathed the girl, hardly believing it.
She remembered that she had not heard a single yelp or bay
in this tunnel, which would have amplified and reechoed any
sound that Nana had made. How the two had come here she
would never know for sure, but it looked as though the dog
had quietly followed the horse until Gem stopped, then
trotted underneath those deadly hooves and sat down before
them to keep the huge beast standing where she was. "I *said*

you were basically responsible," Julie whispered, "but I didn't know how really intelligent you were. Thank you, little beagle."

Had it been Bonnie standing there and shuddering now and again in the cool air, covered with the dark sweat of fright, Julie would have taken the chance of shoving past her, or even, perhaps, of creeping through her legs to the other side. But this mare, a stranger, could literally have crushed the life out of the girl by shifting sideways. Julie was not even certain there would be room to pass if the mare obligingly shoved herself hard against one of the walls.

What if I took a long run and jumped over her tail onto her back? . . .

Oh, no way! That was a fancy cowboy stunt that would send the horse flying forward until both of them were smashed in like a cork into a bottle.

Not under, then; not over, and not beside. How do I get to her head?

There *had* to be a way. This was a poor terrified horse caught far underground and unable to reason out the fact that she had to walk backward to escape. Julie, with a human's logic, must plan for the mare.

She scanned the roof, as uneven here as it had been smooth and featureless behind them. At about shoulder level the place began where the prehistoric collapse had occurred. The walls on either side were gouged in, and the ceiling was high and lumpy. The old river had worked most of the indented places quite smooth, and then its level had fallen— the narrow, shallow little squirt of a brook still went its silent way along the very corner of the floor—so that on either hand as she stood there Julie could see a ledge, about two inches wide on her left, half a foot deep on her right.

She looked at the right shelf. Yes, it went on past the mare's head, but only just past; then it sloped up, and only an insect could have crept along it.

"Good Nana, brave Nana," she said quietly. "Don't you let that mare move a smidgen." Nana kept watching the horse's face intently.

Julie dried her wet palms on her jacket, took a deep breath, and put her hands flat on the strip of stone and shot herself up with all the power of her legs, till she was well above the floor, holding herself stiff-armed on the ledge. She groped with her right foot until she had a precarious toehold, writhed upward, scrambled a moment, and was on the narrow strip of limestone. There was no room to get her hands and feet down on the dangerous perch and move forward in animal fashion. With her feet twisted sideways and her hands clutching at the uneven walls a couple of feet above the shelf on which she stood, Julie began to move on like a human fly across the scooped-out portion of the tunnel, cramped and twisted and scared.

She did her best not to imagine what would happen if she lost her grip and fell onto the horse from this position.

It took forever. She could only progress at the pace of a groggy spider along the terrible little rim. But at last she had reached the end of the ledge and knew that she was just beyond Kimberley Gem's nose—if the horse hadn't stepped forward. There was no way for her to twist her neck and look down, because her body was pressed as close to the concave wall as she could push it. She edged into the most upright position she could manage and let out the deep breath she had taken several hours before—well, it seemed that long!—and inhaled another, and with a quick shove, before she had time to think about it and get petrified with fear, went backward and down.

She lit on her feet, and Kimberley Gem snorted and stepped back a pace. Nana stood up and wagged her tail happily.

First things first: Julie bent and gathered the beagle into a fond hug and murmured praise and endearments lavishly. Nana went delirious with glee. "You poor, dear, brave, smart little thing, and you did it all in the dark," said Julie. "You must have done it by smell and hearing. Oh, such a clever dog!" Then she set the pup on its feet and stood up. Fumbling in a pocket, she found the crumpled remains of several sugar lumps. She held them out on her palm and spoke to the mare and stepped closer. Gem gazed at her, lowered her head, and snuffled up the sweet. Julie eased the halter on and secured it. Then she pulled the leash from her belt and snapped it onto Nana's collar.

"Okay," she said, her voice still shaking with strain, "now we're going to back up for a mile or two."

Gem, it turned out, was not especially happy to back up. Occasionally she stood rock-still and whinnied her disgust at the ordeal, causing echoes such as the cavern had surely never resounded with before. But step by step she went up the gentle slope until, before Julie had any notion how close it was, the opening appeared over the mare's shoulder. They had been hardly more than a hundred yards within the earth.

She and the mare had grown to know each other somewhat. She pushed and shoved and coaxed until Gem, at last becoming used to this curious new gait, confidently went backward without faltering, and they emerged from the mouth of the limestone burrow.

Then, Julie's fist gripping the halter, the mare turned around and progressed in a normal horsey manner toward her stall in Pop Larrikin's stable, with Nana, both the villain and the heroine of the hour, bouncing joyfully along behind.

And now Julie could begin thinking of Bonnie again, and of Pop and Lankes and the unknown, dishonest, possibly evil and threatening Nicholas Grey.

Chapter XIII

Pop watched her over the rim of a cup of buttermilk. "So you know all about it, then," he said sadly.

"Except how you could do it. You're not a crook, Pop. You're a good man who loves horses and—"

"Loves one horse too much, I guess. Sound funny to say I did it for Tweedy? True, though. True as we're sitting here." He sighed and put down the cup. "I had no idea, Julie, when I came here, or for quite a while afterward, what Greyhill Stud was putting over on the others with their big strong foals and high prices. Our mutual pal Leon Pitt is right: you can work part of a farm and never know what in the universe is happening twenty feet away. Guess I was plumb blind for years about it. Never had a hint. Then . . ."

"Yes?"

"Then Bothwell's get started turning out less than magnificent. And I discovered that now mares were in foal to Bothwell who hadn't even *seen* Bothwell. I was his handler, and I knew. So I had it out with Grey, and found out that they'd bred other stallions to those mares, because their get was better than the big fellow's. I was mad clear through. I raved and bellowed. I said I'd quit. Said I'd see that Greyhill was exposed for what it was, a conniving place that . . . And so forth.

"Well, Grey just grinned. Told me I wouldn't, because no one had been hurt—the other studs were fine animals, still are—and I wasn't a man to see dozens of good workers thrown out of jobs. Also, where would I ever find so good a place for Tweedy?"

He got up and walked back and forth on the frayed old rug. "There's no excuse for me, you know. But I slipped. I said all right. I'd go on being Bothwell's handler. And I started breeding my little Scotch Tweed stallion to some of those mares, instead of the other substitutes they usually used for Bothwell."

"You bred Bonnie to him," said Julie huskily.

"Don't jump ahead. This was years ago. I was wrong, but I did it. And the only reason was that I *had* to see Tweedy's destiny as a great sire realized. Naturally, I got nothing out of it, except my normal salary. I'm excusing myself, sorry. No excuse, as I said. However!" He suddenly held up a finger. "I had been right about Tweedy! And that fact kept me going, kept me on here years after I ought to have quit. The place is perfect for him, and he has a chance—a chance nobody but me knows about, mind you, but a chance—to pass along his great qualities."

"You say you'd been right?"

"To date," said Pop solemnly, "and I can prove it, to you anyway, by my records, which I've kept carefully, to date, of the thirteen foals of his that have already reached the track—you listening good and hard?—eleven are already stakes-winning horses, and the other two won three and five races respectively before they were injured and retired from competition! Now, if that isn't an impressive record, justifying my faith in my little fellow, what is?"

"That is amazing." Julie nodded.

"Some of them you know of, I'm sure. Hepburn's Earl, Browneyed Lass, Come On Jimmy—"

"They're Tweedy's?"

"Yep." Pop shook his head. "I figured out the early-foal thing after a while. By then I was all enmeshed in Tweedy's progress as a sire, and, well, I simply ignored everything else." He eyed her mournfully. " 'Tis the tale of an honest man corrupted by love for a fine horse," he said. "Don't mean to joke about it. Feel rotten. Haven't drawn a thoroughly happy breath in years. But if I'd left, they'd have gone right on keeping up Bothwell's reputation with the help of lesser studs, and I kept thinking it was more honest to give owners their foals by Tweedy than by even the excellent studs that were used instead of Bothwell otherwise. Tweedy's presented the track with thirteen grand beasts already, and there are more on their way there. Bothwell in his prime never had a record to equal that."

"What would have happened if you'd just kept breeding Bothwell instead of horses with better sire records?"

"His stud fee would be somewhere around eight thousand instead of eighteen thousand dollars. The foals are worth the money, because the four or five stallions we use are proven sires, and fine ones. Tweedy's best of all. As I knew in my bones that he'd be! But now, how do I prove it? How do I earn him his place in the history books? Why would anyone credit the statement that eleven stakes horses attributed to Bothwell are in fact the get of a crooked-legged, unproven racehorse who never raced?"

He collapsed ino his chair and wheezed, "Nobody would believe it."

"Well, *I* believe it."

"Julie, you know Tweedy, and you have the faith in a horse that some of us do, even without proof, after you've just met him. Some folks call it dumb confidence. I call it horse instinct. But it's unprovable."

"You did breed him to Bonnie, didn't you?"

"That's right. I wasn't about to let any stud but Scotch Tweed sire her first foal. And you can see why, with his record. His secret record."

Julie thought hard for a minute. Then she said, positively, "I'm *glad* you did. Look here, Pop—if we can straighten things out, prove somehow that Tweedy is a terrifically valuable sire, then I'm going to book Bonnie to him. Openly. With publicity. That'll really enhance his appeal to other owners, won't it? Because, after all, Bonnie was the best, the best of the year, and obviously I wouldn't breed her to just any fly-by-night stud."

The bright green eyes pierced her. "You'd really do that? After I went behind your back to do what I did?"

"You did it for good motives!" She remembered something that Leon had said that day. "Worry about a good horse that's in trouble weighs on a man's mind till sometimes he does strange things," she told Pop. "You've paid for the things that have been done here on Greyhill, paid with misery and guilty feelings and unhappiness. And it *did* turn out to be a good thing, because Tweedy's greatness is going to enrich the thoroughbred line forever. So I'd say your record is about balanced now, and—"

"Not quite," said Pop. "I don't want to throw some good fellows out of work, and I surely do not crave to cause a terrible rumpus and uproar. Still. However. Nonetheless. I have to stop this Bothwell-substitute racket before more bloodlines are tangled than can ever be put right. I've had enough of the double-dealing, and some of the lads on the farm feel the same. My helper, youngster you saw with me today, he's about ready to let his conscience take over and talk to the Jockey Club. Fact is, anybody halfway decent on the place is up to his craw with the dirty work."

"Inspector Vickel told me that 'the game was about played out,' " said Julie.

"Who? Have you spoken to the police?"

"No, that's what I call the gate guard. Don't tell me his real name," said Julie hastily, "I'd rather think of him that way."

Pop blinked. "You're enigmatically inclined today. Right. Forward. I have to tell Grey that, as your friends says, the game's played out. Not vindictive, you understand. Just coming to action after too many years of sliding along. Now, then. He's liable to see that an accident happens to me. I want you to take Tweedy away from here, if you will, and Kimberley Gem. House 'em for me at Fieldstone—I think Leon Pitt would do that for an old friend."

"He'll do more than that. He told me he needed a good stud groom, and he was hinting at you when he said it. And Mr. T doesn't have a top-quality stallion at the moment, because we retired our best one due to age, and two that he was dickering for just turned out to be not as perfect as he'd thought, and—"

"You saying that Tolkov might be interested in having Tweedy as his principal stud?"

"When we've proved his record."

"How?"

"We'll find a way."

"We will?"

"Yep."

"You sound like me."

"It's contagious."

"Ah, yes!"

They stared at each other and chuckled. Then Julie said seriously, "Are you really going to be in danger?"

"No notion. Grey is tough, and Lenkes is tougher. And they're both mean."

"Why don't you come along with me and the horses, then, without telling them anything?"

"A man can't crawl away like that, Julie."

"It seems to me a man has to do some very dumb things, then, considering they're mean and tough and at least two to one against a man," grumbled the girl.

"A man might have to recover his honor in his own eyes," said Pop mildly.

"Oh, all right. But will you come to Fieldstone afterward? Leon will give you that job, I know it; he as much as said so. And bring all your records on Tweedy."

"Wait." Pop darted over to a beat-up desk in the corner and pulled out several stacks of papers. He dropped these into a disreputable briefcase, gazed around, added his pair of cut-back blinkers and more papers, and finally a few items that Julie did not notice, old and cherished mementos of his early years at the track. "You have a van, you said. You can carry this with you. It's all I'll worry about in case I have to take off flying, as the saying goes. I can come back for my books, if they don't burn the house down out of pique."

"Last time I saw the van, it had two wheels hanging over a hay field. Inspector Vickel was going to send tractors to save it, but I don't know whether he did."

"Let's go see. I want to whistle up Delia, too. She can go with you?" he asked anxiously.

"Oh, Pop, of course!" She felt herself close to tears. "I feel as if I'm abandoning you to a horrible f-fate."

"Nonsense. Balderdash." He shrugged on an ancient fleece-lined jacket. "Ready?"

"Yes." She trailed him miserably to the door and waited as he gave a final look around the snug room. Then they were outside, and Pop was carefully locking the house up behind them, while a sleepy Nana on the end of her leash blinked at the late afternoon.

As they walked up the road side by side, she told Pop how Kimberley Gem had run away and been brought back. "She's all right. I got her dry and comfy, and she's really a friendly soul, because she kissed me on the cheek twice."

"You're certain Leon can keep the two of 'em at Fieldstone for a while, even if I don't turn up?"

"Why wouldn't you turn up? You think they're going to *murder* you?" said Julie.

"Oh, for the love of mud and briers! At the most they'll swat me around a little, thinking they'll change my mind. But they can't do that. I've spent time in hospitals with busted jaws and cracked ribs before. It isn't all that big a deal. You forget about it. I'm asking, if worst comes to worst, can Leon—"

"We must have twenty empty stalls at Fieldstone, and

thirty at Deepwater. I'll take care of Tweedy and Gem myself."

"You're quite a girl," he said with approval. "Knew it the
day you walked in here."

Inspector Vickel, rather to Julie's surprise, had been as
good as his word, and had not wasted time about sending the
tractors; for the Fieldstone van stood waiting for them in the
middle of the hogback. Julie and Pop got in with Nana and
trundled down the road and up the rise, then in to Pop's
stable. Together they led first Tweedy and then the mare out
and up into the van, secured them in the stalls, and barred
the double doors.

"I'm going across to the office now," said Pop, rubbing
his button nose. "Make better time afoot. You go collect
Sunbonnet. Maybe I'll pick you up at the gate, maybe not. If
I'm not there, go on without me. You'll have to favor
Tweedy's bad leg, and drive pretty slowly."

"I will. How about Delia?"

He shook his head. "I'd forget my left foot if it wasn't
glued on!" He gave a piercing whistle, waited a moment, then
repeated it. Shortly the little brown-and-white hound appeared from the nearest patch of woods, lolloping along toward them. Pop welcomed her and leashed her. "Go with
Julie, girl. Remember, she's the boss."

The two dogs greeted each other happily on the floor of
the cab. Julie got behind the wheel. Pop waved briskly at her
and started out straight across the field toward the office,
which was a small brick one-room building a short distance
beyond the main gate. He had some up-and-down traveling to
do, but at his quick stride he would arrive there before
Julie could reach the barn.

She reversed and moved the van slowly out to the road,
turned, and started north. She took the hogback at a snail's
pace, and followed her previous route as well as she could
recollect it, but made a wrong turning and had to backtrack,
so that when she came to the barren-mare barns, nearly
twenty minutes had elapsed.

There were half a dozen men standing there waiting for
her. Julie had been fretting over the fact that she had not
told Pop about her lack of a gate pass for Bonnie. Now it
struck her that she should have also told him how extremely
timid she felt in the presence of the large and threatening
stablemen of Greyhill. There was the man who had refused

to let her take Bonnie away without a pass. There, looking taller than ever, with a heavy scowl between his eyes and a sullen droop to his moustache, stood Robert Lenkes. There were four thick-muscled strangers.

And here was Julie, a slim eighteen-year-old girl with two contraband horses in the back, two dogs and a briefcase full of valuable and irreplaceable data beside her, and a heavy lump of ice in her stomach.

"Guard, Nana," she said rather hopelessly to her beagle, and parked the van and got out, closing the door behind her.

Lenkes was the one to speak to. He was the manager, after all, and she knew him. Even though he *did* look the maddest of the lot.

"I came for Sunbonnet," she said, stopping in front of him and tipping her head to look him in the eye.

"We've been expecting you. What's Larrikin been telling you?"

Pop had already had it out with them, then. Where was he? "Nothing I hadn't found out already," said Julie, her voice shaking and a little high. "Nothing that Monty Everett didn't guess and that Leon Pitt, and probably Mr. Tolkov, doesn't know by now."

His eyebrows went up. He said something under his breath. "I don't believe you."

"Then you're not very bright," said Julie. "Monty and I saw those early foals. Some of your people here talk more than they would if they were really happy about your operation. It was *me* told *Pop* about the whole thing, and if you ask him, he'll admit it. He didn't have to tell me anything."

"And what do you think you're going to do with your so-called information?"

"Are you saying that it isn't real information?"

"I'm saying you have no proof."

"Proof of what?"

Lenkes glared at her, a little less sure of himself. "The early foals," he said shortly.

"And the false affidavits on Bothwell's being the sire of so many stakes winners."

"That too. Larrikin lied to you."

"No, he didn't! I heard about it all *before* I mentioned it to him!" She shook her head, baffled anew. "Did you really think nobody would ever tell? Your days of cheating the racing fraternity are over, Mr. Lenkes, and you know it.

Your security systems had all kinds of leaks in it. If you hadn't been so dumb and sure of yourselves," she went on in spite of herself, because she was angry, "you'd have seen to it that nobody from Deepwater or any of the other big farms ever got onto this place without at least two smart men to guard them! We chased my puppy into that barn perfectly innocently, and there were those November foals hidden away. You finally got just too *stupid* about everything! Well, I've told Leon Pitt, and Monty's told Mr. Tolkov, or soon will; and if Mr. Rollin Tolkov doesn't go to the Jockey Club right away when he—"

"Well, Lenkes," said one of the other men in a resigned tone, "she's right. That blows it sky-high. It's all finished."

"Shut up, Bill."

"Why? What do you think you're gonna do, convince this kid that she doesn't know what she knows?" The man put a hand on Lenkes's shoulder. "If it was only Larrikin, we could maybe hush it up. But Tolkov!"

"This girl isn't Tolkov, by a long shot."

"What are you gonna do, then, pay her off? You look at that chin on her and them eyes," said the man reasonably, "and tell me you can persuade her to tell Tolkov she was wrong."

Lenkes regarded Julie with so venomous a gaze that she could feel her hair curling at the ends. "I'll think of something," he said coldly.

"If you lay one hand on me, you will wind up in jail," said Julie as steadily as she was able. "I'm going to get Sunbonnet."

"Go ahead, kid," said one of the other men; she was startled to see that it was the stablehand who had stopped her earlier. "He ain't gonna touch you."

"Won't I?" said Lenkes, flexing his big hands. "She's going to bust up this place, put every one of us out of work, get me barred from the track for life, and some of you too, and I'm going to stand here and *let* her?"

"Yes, you are," said Julie.

"You sure are," said the man called Bill. "Late registration of foals is kind of harmless, if you ask me, and usin' better studs than Bothwell is even doin' the owners a favor. But if you start roughing people up, and especially if you try to hurt a girl, well, brother, you'll be smeared all over the side of this barn before you know what hit you."

"You talk big for a guy who just lost his job," said Lenkes.

"I talk sense. The Jockey Club can close us down. But ain't none of us here ever spent a night in jail, and we don't intend to, not for you and Grey."

The others murmured agreement. Julie said, "Thank you, gentlemen," and walked around Lenkes and into the barn.

Bonnie greeted her loudly. She had probably heard Julie's voice outside, and wondered when she would come in. Julie patted her and put the Deepwater halter on her, then led her slowly out of the stable door.

"I wasn't going to hurt her," Lenkes was saying. "I was going to talk sense to her."

"And another thing," said Bill, who evidently was seething with long-subdued resentments, "Pop Larrikin's been a good buddy to every man here, and if you've hurt him, you're gonna wish you hadn't got out of bed this morning."

"Oh, dry up and blow away!" shouted Lenkes. "He's down at the office this minute, chewing out Grey! You think Grey's going to hurt him? What kind of nut are you?"

"The kind of nut who saw you just almost take a swing at a child, and a female to boot," roared Bill. "I tell you, that kid's got nerve you'd sell your shirt for. Takes a lot to face up to six grown men and tell 'em they're out in the cold and she's done it. She was scared chalk-white, but she told you the plain truth. Lenkes," he said, suddenly quiet, "you make me sick. Go groom a colt or something."

"Yeah, said two of the others simultaneously, and a third added, "Think I'll slide down to the office and resign, and see if Pop's okay."

"If he'd hit a girl, he'd take a hammer to Pop Larrikin," said someone. "I'll go too."

"We'll all go," said Lenkes. "I'll show you your pal Larrikin's all in one piece." He made a noise of utter disgust. "What a bunch of old maids," he said.

Julie had opened the doors of the van and put down the ramp. Now she led Bonnie up and into the third stall. She secured the great bay filly and gave her a carrot that she'd found in her jacket, and began to close up the van. The man Bill was abruptly beside her, helping with the ramp and doors. "It's all right, Miss Jefferson," he said to her, smiling, "it's only what we ought to have done years ago. Lenkes won't hurt you."

"I wasn't at all sure of that," said Julie gratefully.

"I could see," he told her. "Your face was the color of a rich man's Sunday shirt. Well, good luck," he said awkwardly.

She shook hands with him. "Same to you, Bill, and thanks."

She got into the cab and closed the door. Her hands were shaking with relief. Inevitably she ground the gears, but she got rolling, and in a few moments pulled up in front of the office. She gave her horn a tap. Pop Larrikin appeared, looking like a leprechaun who had just had a fight with a toad over who owned a particular mushroom: belligerent, red in the face, rather swollen with anger, and a little surprised to find himself undamaged.

"You want a passenger, lady?"

"Love one, Pop."

He went around to the other side and hopped in, reshuffling the dogs in order to put his feet down comfortably. "You got her all right, then."

"I did. You told off Grey and Lenkes."

"I did. Lenkes looked mean and went off to see about you, but Grey just sort of shriveled and sank into himself. I think he's been expecting this for a long time. You never saw such a guilty conscience show so plain." He relaxed with a sigh. "That's that." Then he was bolt upright and staring through the windshield. "Oh-oh! That isn't quite that."

The gates ahead were shut, and five or six men stood in a line before them.

"That's bad news," said Pop slowly. "Those are the mean guys."

"Who?"

"The bonus fellows. The boys who stand to lose not just jobs, but double-pay jobs. Julie, what have I let you in for?"

Chapter XIV

Julie Jefferson eased the van to a halt just short of the ominously waiting men. They looked vicious, and she was far more afraid of them than she had been of Lenkes, for they seemed a much less disciplined and more irresponsible pack of men than the ordinary stablehands who'd been backing the manager. She dried her hands on her jeans and tried not to look as vulnerable as she felt.

"Pop, I'm a girl, and they won't hurt me. You stay in the cab—"

"I will not!"

"You will! Someone has to keep the dogs safe." She said hastily, hoping he wouldn't argue, "Please, please, stay in here." Then she swung her door open and jumped down and slammed it behind her.

"Where you goin', little girl?" asked the obvious leader harshly, and then grinned around at the others as though he were quite a wit.

"Out," said Julie. "I know, Lenkes sent the word around that I was going to tell the authorities all about your schemes. Well, I am. You haven't got anything to lose more than you've lost already, unless you try to hurt me. Then you're in *real* trouble."

"You gonna hurt me?" said the leader, and reaching out, he caught her by the arm. "How about if I push that pretty nose into your face?"

It was like a scene from an old movie on TV. Julie could not believe it. But not one of the others made a move or raised an objection.

"That will only put you in jail," she said, her voice cracking. Her whole being cried out to her to shriek, to wrench away and run back toward the distant Bill and his friends. With one of the biggest efforts of her life, she remained absolutely still.

"I been in jail before," said the man. "It ain't so bad. Besides, can I help it if you fall down and mash up your face? Now, you're gonna listen to reason."

"I can listen to reason till midnight," said Julie, "but it won't change my mind."

"Then I got to be a little rough," he said. And his face convinced her that he would.

Pop was out of the van and storming toward them from the other side, and one of the other men had stepped in front of him and was about to throw a punch. Julie saw this out of the corner of her eye and said loudly, "Pop, please! He doesn't *dare* hurt me." She wished that she could believe that herself. Gathering the last scraps of her courage, turning her head away from the gauntlet of hard stares and clenching fists, she said, "Take your silly hand off me and open the gates. Have some sense. Do you know how many years you can get for manhandling a girl?"

"I'll get a good lawyer," he said, but his grip loosened slightly. "Why don't you be smart and gimme your word that you won't—"

"I've already told several people what's going on at Grey-hill. You might as well quit." She felt strange, as though she were going to pass out. She focused her gaze intently right between his narrowed eyes. He began to blink. Nerves. He was bluffing her. She found herself breathing almost normally. "Let go," she said.

"Slap her silly, Joe," said someone.

"Don't be a fool, Joe," said Pop, who was being held by a man twice his size. "And you, Tom, that goes for you too."

"Robert Lenkes gave up," said Julie steadily. "He'll tell you that when he gets here. Nicholas Grey caved in. *He* won't back you up. Take your hand away." She continued to stare at him. "Besides," she said, "you smell just terrible, and you're making me a little ill."

One or two of the men, serious and angered though they were, laughed aloud, and one said, "Old bathless Joe!"

The face before her seemed to inflate and darken. She had struck him on a sore spot, and what common sense he had was gone. He lifted his free hand.

"Aarrghhh!" said a tremendous voice behind her. "You, Joe, you reeking maniac, what are you doing to that girl?" And into the horrible, tense moment there erupted the short and brawny form of Inspector Vickel.

"Minute I turn my back!" he howled. "Grabbing at people! Stopping vickels! My job, not yours, to stop vickels! Orrgh!"

He gave a sort of semi-karate chop to Joe's arm, and the fingers that held Julie went limp and dropped away from her. Joe turned on the guard with a snarl of pain and rage. Then a fist sank into his middle, and what happened for some minutes thereafter was of no interest whatever to him.

"Sorry about that, Miss Jefferson," said the inspector. He rounded on the others. "You, you bunch of overpaid exercise boys, you know that this girl saved my life today? Took me off a absolute cliff where I was going to fall in and break my spine?" He evidently considered it of no importance that Julie had accidentally put him into the position from which she had "saved" him. Inspector Vickel had more intelligence than she had credited to him. He began to rave at the others. He ordered Pop released, and Pop was released. He demanded that they disperse, and with sullen looks and grumblings they dispersed a few steps. Lifting his fists and his voice, he called upon heaven to witness that they were a pack of worthless, toothless curs, while Julie was a real thoroughbred who'd faced them down like the many whelps they were; and they stared at him under their brows and evidently did their best to live up to his description.

Then Lenkes and the five others arrived, and there was much arguing and shouting, but any danger was now quite plainly gone, and Julie walked over to Pop and said, "I guess we can go now."

"After I shake a few hands," said Pop, and mingled in the crowd, doing so. Julie herself clasped the hand of Inspector Vickel and thanked him, at which he snorted and said under his breath, "You said you wouldn't blab it around that I told you what I did. That's kind. That's thoughtful. I couldn't let that dope Joe hurt you."

Soon they were ready to leave. "Pop," said Julie, aware of weakness in her knees and elbows, "I think you'd better drive."

"Right." They got into the van, trying not to step on two hysterical little dogs. Inspector Vickel himself opened the gates for them, and the last Julie saw of him, he was standing squarely in the center of the big driveway, waving cordially.

"I really thought he was kind of foolish," Julie said, "but Inspector Vickel isn't at all. He handled those men marvelously."

"He isn't a bad fellow. Suppose you tell me where you got that name for him."

Julie did. Pop laughed. "First time I let out a happy sound today," he said. "And jollier than Grey and Lenkes will feel for many a long week."

"What will happen, Pop?"

"Well, I think I can predict that. First off, young Everett and you and I, maybe with my friend Buck, will go to the Jockey Club and tell them everything we know. Greyhill Stud will be discredited as a breeding farm; that's to say, once the big sales companies, like Fasig-Tipton, realize that their foals have been misrepresented, they won't accept yearlings from Greyhill anymore. So long as it's owned by Grey and managed by Lenkes and company."

"What about all those horses? What about Bothwell?"

"Well, this business doesn't detract from the value of the stock. It only means that a new management is in order. Grey will have to sell. It goes without saying that he and Lenkes, and certainly Joe, the brute who wanted to swat you, are through forever at the track. The others will find jobs, I think. I'll personally vouch for Buck. He was my helper, big young fellow you saw with Bonnie this morning. Good lad. Bothwell? I imagine someone will buy him and see if a reduced book will bring back his value as a sire."

He rubbed his chin. "You sure Leon had me in mind when he said he needed a stud groom?"

"He as much as said so."

"He didn't know how deep I was in sin."

"You have nothing to worry about," said Julie, finally relaxing and slumping back against the seat. "You redeemed yourself. Besides, you didn't hurt anyone, you helped. With Tweedy."

"Tweedy. Yes. Ah. Tweedy . . ."

"Leon needs a stud groom, Mr. T needs a top stud. That takes care of both of you. With Tweedy's record, it's a cinch."

"Tweedy's record isn't official."

"I'll bet we can make it official." The girl had had an inspiration. "Blood tests! Not very long ago someone proved that the sire of two colts, who couldn't possibly have been the sire, *was* the sire." She stopped and listened to an instant replay of that sentence in her head. "I guess you know what I mean. Anyway, they used blood tests, and the Jockey Club accepted them."

"Yes, I remember that."

"Well, you have complete records of the foals that Tweedy sired. You can provide your sworn affidavits and Buck's too that Tweedy was the sire, show them your records, and with the blood tests on the horses in question—yay! Scotch Tweed is the wonder of the world."

Pop squinted thoughtfully down the highway. "Hmm. You know, it might work out. It just might."

"It will," said Julie, "because it has to."

"If it does, then the Jockey Club will issue new registration certificates on all the horses involved, and with Sunbonnet booked to Tweedy, by George!" said Pop, "I believe we'll be in business."

"What about all the other horses who—"

"I was coming to that when Tweedy sidetracked me. I imagine that the Jockey Club will soon realize there's no way they can possibly ever know which foals have had falsified foaling dates and which have been given untrue stallion certificates. I'm certain that my records on Tweedy are the only ones that anybody kept, and even Lenkes could never remember all of the data. So I'd predict that the Jockey Club will ultimately throw up its collective hands and say that they can only go 'from this day forward' with matters as they stand."

He was silent for a while, as the van rolled smoothly under his experienced hands down the highway toward Fieldstone Farm. "Grey is going to be smacked with lawsuits by the carload," he said at last. "I don't envy him. But he deserves it." Pop glanced at her. "You do know that I only made salary? I never accepted a bonus or took a bribe."

"Oh, Pop, I know that!"

"How?"

"Character. Shines in your eyes," she said, imitating him. "I can tell. Met enough crooks in my time to recognize one when I see him. You're honest. Misguided. But honest." She broke up in giggles. "I probably sound like somebody on a TV show, but I mean it, honestly."

Half the journey now passed without a word between them. But a tangible air of friendship filled the cab of the horse van. Nana crawled up on Julie's lap and went to sleep with a small sigh of weariness. Delia bedded herself down on the girl's feet. Finally Pop cleared his throat and said, "Penny."

"What?"

"Penny for your thoughts. You're a million miles away."

"No, just back there a few feet," said Julie. "With Bonnie and Tweedy and Gem."

"What are you thinking?"

"About what to name the foal. 'Sunbonnet' and 'Scotch Tweed.' That should make something like 'Bonnie Dundee.' Or 'Dundee Bonnet.' "

Pop thought awhile and then asked, "How about 'Deerstalker'?"

"How do you get that?"

"Cap, like Sherlock Holmes used to wear. Made of tweed."

"Lots of possibilities," said Julie drowsily. "But I know one thing for sure: whatever I call it, it will be a marvelous foal."

"A world-beater."

"The best foal in the entire universe!" said Julie Jefferson.